Emily Harvale lives i
– although she wou
French Alps ... or Canada ... or anywhere that
has several months of snow. Emily loves
snow almost as much as she loves Christmas.
Having worked in the City (London) for
several years, Emily returned to her home
town of Hastings where she spends her days
writing ... and wondering if it will ever snow.
You can contact her via her website,
Facebook or Instagram.
There is also a Facebook group where fans
can chat with Emily about her books, her
writing day and life in general. Details can be
found on Emily's website.

Author contacts:
www.emilyharvale.com
www.twitter.com/emilyharvale
www.facebook.com/emilyharvalewriter
www.instagram.com/emilyharvale

***

Scan the code above to see all Emily's books on
Amazon

Also by this author

The Golf Widows' Club
Sailing Solo
Carole Singer's Christmas
Christmas Wishes
A Slippery Slope
The Perfect Christmas Plan
Be Mine
It Takes Two
Bells and Bows on Mistletoe Row

Lizzie Marshall series:
Highland Fling – book 1
Lizzie Marshall's Wedding – book 2

Goldebury Bay series:
Ninety Days of Summer – book 1
Ninety Steps to Summerhill – book 2
Ninety Days to Christmas – book 3

Hideaway Down series:
A Christmas Hideaway – book 1
Catch A Falling Star – book 2
Walking on Sunshine – book 3
Dancing in the Rain – book 4

Hall's Cross series
Deck the Halls – book 1
The Starlight Ball – book 2

Michaelmas Bay series
Christmas Secrets in Snowflake Cove – book 1
Blame it on the Moonlight – book 2

Lily Pond Lane series
The Cottage on Lily Pond Lane – four-part serial
Part One – New beginnings
Part Two – Summer secrets
Part Three – Autumn leaves

Part Four – Trick or treat
Christmas on Lily Pond Lane
Return to Lily Pond Lane
A Wedding on Lily Pond Lane
Secret Wishes and Summer Kisses on Lily Pond Lane

Wyntersleap series
Christmas at Wynter House – Book 1
New Beginnings at Wynter House – Book 2
A Wedding at Wynter House – Book 3
Love is in the Air – spin off

Merriment Bay series
Coming Home to Merriment Bay – Book 1
(four-part serial)
Part One – A Reunion
Part Two – Sparks Fly
Part Three ~ Christmas
Part Four – Starry Skies
Chasing Moonbeams in Merriment Bay – Book 2
Wedding Bells in Merriment Bay – Book 3

Seahorse Harbour series
Summer at my Sister's – book 1
Christmas at Aunt Elsie's – book 2
Just for Christmas – book 3
Tasty Treats at Seahorse Bites Café – book 4
Dreams and Schemes at The Seahorse Inn – book 5
Weddings and Reunions in Seahorse Harbour – book 6

Clementine Cove series
Christmas at Clementine Cove – book 1
Broken Hearts and Fresh Starts at Cove Café – book 2
Friendships Blossom in Clementine Cove – book 3

Norman Landing series
Saving Christmas – book 1
A not so secret Winter Wedding – book 2
Sunsets and surprises at Seascape Café-book 3
A Date at the end of The Pier – book 4

ISBN 978-1-909917-91-0

Published by Crescent Gate Publishing

Print edition published worldwide 2023
E-edition published worldwide 2023

Cover design by JR and Emily Harvale

Emily Harvale

A Summer Escape

CRESCENT GATE PUBLISHING

Acknowledgements

My grateful thanks go to the following:

My webmaster, David Cleworth who does so much more than website stuff.
My cover design team, JR.
Luke Brabants. Luke is a talented artist and can be found at: www.lukebrabants.com
My wonderful friends for their friendship and love. You know I love you all.
All the fabulous members of my Readers' Club. You help and support me in so many ways and I am truly grateful for your ongoing friendship. I wouldn't be where I am today without you.
My Twitter and Facebook friends, and fans of my Facebook author page. It's great to chat with you. You help to keep me (relatively) sane!

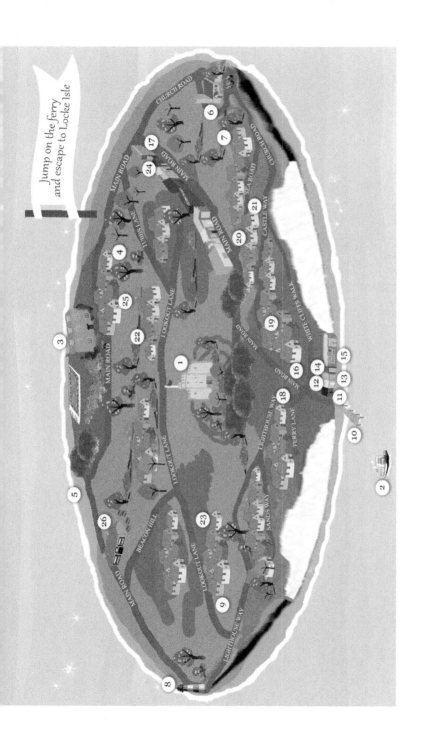

Jump on the ferry and escape to Locke Isle

MAP KEY – LOCKE ISLE

1. **Locke Keep** – The castle-like home of Ward Locke. His ancestors had owned Locke Isle and everything on it for centuries, but his grandfather and father have sold certain properties to the residents over the last hundred years.
2. **Locke Isle Ferry** – owned and operated by Ward Locke.
3. **Castle Keep Hotel** – luxury hotel (and former Mansion House home of Ward's Aunt Agatha) owned by Ward Locke but managed by Tristan Goldsby. The hotel is the place to go for the Spa and the heated pool.
4. **Frenchman's Cottage** - Tristan Goldsby, the manager of Castle Keep Hotel lives here
5. **Frenchman's Cove** – this is the beach adjoining the hotel.
6. **Church of St Mary on the Water** – The Reverend Minton Bloom is the vicar. He's in his 70s and hard of hearing but he's determined to remain in post.
7. **Land's End House** – the Rectory

8. **The Lighthouse** – it still functions and does an important job in keeping the heavy traffic in the English Channel away from the island and the rocks.

9. **Lookout Cottage** - this is where the lighthouse keeper, Jonas Barnaby lives with his wife Nell.

10. **Boardwalk** – part of this structure juts out to sea and it's where the ferry docks, and part is on dry land and is a promenade with a small parade of shops and a café.

11. **Locke Isle Tourist Office** – It's the first building you reach on Boardwalk, has a purple-painted façade ... and always seems to be closed.

12. **Duponts -** Frederick Dupont – Tailor, and his wife Esther Dupont – Dressmaker, work here but they live in the aptly named, Haberdasher's Cottage. The shop front is brightly painted, yellow and green.

13. **Buds and Blooms**, - is the florist shop, painted orange, and owned and run by Bernie (Bernadette) Burns, a widow for three years.

14. **White Cliffs Café** – is painted

blue. It is owned and run by two sisters, Sylvia (Sylvie) Shaw, the youngest, and Celia Thatcher (Cece) the eldest. They are both in their fifties, and single, although Cece is a widow. They also have an older brother, Alfred, who has been a widower for ten years but he's always had a soft spot for Bernie, the florist.

15. **Locke's Convenience Store** – owned by Ward's, Aunt Agatha (Aggie)

16. **White Cliffs Cottage** – home to Tracy (65) and Roger White (80) it's close to the cliff edge, although not as close as some of the other properties on the island. Roger was the ferryman all his life until he retired at 79 Tracy and Roger met on the ferry and they've been married for 20 years. Tracy was Geneva's nanny from the day of Geneva's birth until she was 8, when Tracy was sacked.

17. **The Clothing Locker** –It's owned by Agatha Locke, Ward's aunt, but Natalie Harte runs it.

18. **Bluebell Cottage** – Bernie Burns lives here

19. **Honeysuckle Cottage** – Alfred

Shaw lives here

20. **Magpie Cottage** – Cece Thatcher lives here

21. **Wren Cottage** – Sylvie Shaw lives here

22. **Haberdasher's Cottage** – home to Frederick Dupont and his wife Esther.

23. **Lockekeep Cottage** – home to Ward's aunt, Agatha Locke (Aggie)

24. **Fifi's Cuisine** – French restaurant on Main Road

25. **Croft Cottage** – Natalie Harte lives here with her young daughter, and her mum. The father of Natalie's child ran off and joined the Navy and hasn't been seen since. He lived in Folkestone. Natalie works in The Clothing Locker and her mum looks after the child.

26. **The Beacon Inn** – the only pub on the island (although there is a bar in Castle Keep Hotel) Owned by Ward Locke but licensed to Harry Flight, who lives here with his wife June, their son, Roman and their daughter, Alana.

Wish you were here?

This new series is set on Locke Isle, a fictional island two miles off the Kent coast, and also partly in the real town of Folkestone, but I have added a few fictional things/places/businesses in Folkestone – like the slipway where the Locke Isle Ferry docks, among others, so please forgive me for that!

In addition to this, my other new series, Betancourt Bay which links to this Locke Isle series, is also set in a fictional village a mile from Folkestone. I've, sort of, 'demolished' everything that currently occupies this space in real life, and 'built' Betancourt Bay there instead. Apologies for that, but it was a necessary evil in order for me to tell these stories.

So if you know Folkestone and the surrounding area, you may not entirely recognise it when you read these books.....

With love,
Emily xx

To twin sisters, Kitty and Anne.
Happy BIG birthday to you both.
I hope your own Summer Escape is fantastic!
Love and best wishes for your special day. xx

One

'Taking a break!' Dad roars, repeating my last three words as if they are a foreign language and he can't comprehend what they mean. I knew he wouldn't be pleased by my decision, but sonic booms make less noise. I'm surprised the floor-to-ceiling windows in his spacious penthouse office haven't shattered. But the glass is toughened. A bit like me.

Other people would be quaking in their shoes, including Mum. I remain composed. Or as composed as I can be, now he's cut short my hastily rehearsed and somewhat lengthy speech. His face is the colour of the sumptuous crimson leather sofa on which we're sitting.

A sofa is not Dad's happy place. Sofas are for relaxing and Dad does not relax. This sofa is here because the office designer said it would make the vast space less echoey, when

Dad had this towering office block redecorated ten years ago. If she had said it would give the office a more homely feel, both the sofa and the designer would have been thrown out.

Dad glowers at me, his fists clenching and unclenching as though he's tempted to lash out. But that's something Dad won't do. He may be tough; he may be ruthless; he may be cruel with both words and deeds, but he's not a physically violent man.

I cough to clear my throat, yet when I speak, it sounds as if I've swallowed a mouse; all I can do is squeak. 'Yes, Dad.' So much for remaining composed. I inhale deeply and try again. 'I'm taking a break.'

He jumps to his feet and marches towards his matching leather executive chair, stopping momentarily as two ravens soar past the expanse of glass. Dad harrumphs at them and continues to his chair; I watch in silence for a few seconds as they perform their aerial acrobatics and then swoop down towards the street, several storeys below.

What does it feel like to be that free? I doubt I'll ever know.

Many people believe ravens bring illness, loss, bad fortune or even death; others that they are a symbol of rebirth and starting anew. I'm going with the latter, obviously. Dad's possibly leaning towards the first. Or more likely, neither. Dad isn't one for superstition and has no time for omens.

He spins round, glares at me with ice in his eyes, and drops into his chair behind his gargantuan, walnut desk.

'We're McBriars, girl!' There's contempt in his tone and in his eyes and the sneer on his face tells me more than any words could, no matter how loudly they are shouted. Although his voice is an octave lower now he's sitting in his chair, dominating the room once more, just the way he likes it. 'We don't "take breaks".'

I shut my eyes for a nanosecond to bolster my confidence. I knew this would not be easy but I had hoped Dad would give me a chance to explain.

I had to virtually beg him to come and sit beside me on the sofa, although I was rather surprised when he did. Sitting opposite him at his desk would automatically have put me at a disadvantage. His massive chair is slightly raised, while the smaller chairs opposite are slightly lowered, so that Dad is looking down on anyone unfortunate enough to be seated across the desk from him. I hoped that sitting on the sofa, would make my news seem more informal, like any normal daughter telling her dad she needs to take a break from work for a while to think things through, and to re-evaluate her life and her priorities.

But Dad and I are not a normal dad and daughter and we do not have the sort of relationship where we sit side by side on a sofa and chat. For one thing, we're exceedingly wealthy, thanks mainly to Dad's thriving property empire, built by him from scratch almost fifty years before, but Mum's career as a supermodel has also added considerable cash to the family coffers. I've worked for Dad from the moment I left university and due to receiving a good salary, and making some wise investments, I've built up a substantial bank balance of my own. For another thing, I no longer live at the family home, McBriar House, I have my own apartment in Edinburgh city centre.

Even when I lived at home we never sat together. Dad has his own chair in the sitting room of McBriar House. It resembles a throne, much like the one in *Game of Thrones*, only with an exceptionally comfortable and luxurious, padded seat and back rest. It was custom-made and the iron work is exquisite ... and also a little terrifying at first sight. Just as it is meant to be. Just like my dad.

I do miss living in that house. It's a palatial eight-bedroom sandstone building, in the Scots Baronial style, and was a former country family seat dating from the 1600s, before Dad bought it for a fortune – although a lot less than the guide price – soon after he married Mum, forty years ago. It wasn't called McBriar House back then, of course. Dad changed its name and removed all trace of its former owners. It's six miles south-west of Edinburgh and sits on seven and a half acres of land with designer gardens, woodland, a swimming pool, a tennis court, and a river running through its grounds. It now also has a Heli-pad, thanks to Dad. I've seen some magnificent houses over the years, but McBriar House is still one of the most beautiful homes I've ever seen. Dad bought it because it is less than twenty minutes away from both Edinburgh International Airport, and also the city centre and the towering office block that's home to McBriar Properties. Mum's career meant she was constantly flying off somewhere, usually to an exotic location, so the close proximity to the airport was handy for her.

I moved out in my twenties because I needed my own space, and somewhere I could take a boyfriend without fear of him running into Dad, and facing an interrogation that would make the Spanish Inquisition seem like playful kittens. Not that I've had that many boyfriends, and only one who really mattered. Only one I fell in love with.

But I'm trying not to think about Mackenzie Fisher.

Although, in truth, he's one of the reasons I need to take this break.

I can't recall the last time Dad and I did sit side by side before today, apart from at someone's wedding, or a funeral, or at another desk in one of the conference rooms in McBriar Tower, negotiating a big deal.

Everything about my dad is 'big'. Big office, big business, big voice, big build, big personality and, several people might say, big bully.

Dad narrows his eyes and slowly leans back in his chair. I know that move. I've seen it hundreds of times. He thinks he's won. But he's in for a surprise.

'Technically, I'm only half McBriar, Dad. Mum's a McBriar by marriage.' I grin warily. 'Fortunately.'

'If that's an attempt at humour, you'd better try again.'

'No. I'm merely pointing out that as half of me comes from Mum, you shouldn't be surprised. Mum's been on a semi-permanent 'break' for years.'

'What your mother does is of no concern to you, girl.' His tone is glacial now. 'Don't push me, I warn you.'

I could argue that, as her only daughter, what Mum does should concern me, but the truth is Dad's right. I gave up trying to get her attention long before I reached my teens, so what she does or where she is, has negligible impact on me now. I know that she's in Cannes at the moment staying with some friends, because I read it in the papers, just like everyone else. I read that news online, Dad no doubt read it in one of the printed versions fanned out before him on the table at breakfast. That's his usual routine, although Mum may have told him herself. She didn't bother to tell me. One thing we all agree on though, is we're all happier these days when Mum and Dad are apart.

'I let you have your way with that Norman Landing deal,' Dad continues. 'Don't think that because I agreed to back away from that, I'm getting soft. I did so simply because it made good business sense. No point in throwing good money after bad.'

I bristle at his words, reminded once again of Mack.

'Soft is not a word I would ever use to describe you, Dad. But this is good business sense too. My head is all over the place right now and as you are well aware, my heart was recently broken.'

His derisive snort of laughter stops me

momentarily. 'That was almost two months ago. And I told you that would happen. Any fool could see that man wasn't in love with you. Pull yourself together and find a way to get revenge. That'll do you far more good than this ridiculous 'break' idea.'

'It's not revenge I want! I want time to deal with my feelings. Time to decide where I go from here.'

'Feelings? Get a grip, Geneva! And where you go from here is onwards and upwards. What you don't do is run away and lick your wounds. You don't let that man win.'

'It's not about winning, Dad. That's the thing. I don't see this as running away. I see it as taking a step towards a better me. A happier future.'

'A better you? A happier future? Have you lost your mind?'

'No. But if I don't take a break, I think I might. I don't expect you to understand. But believe me when I say I need this, Dad. I need this break. Please don't fight me. Give me a few weeks. A month. Or possibly two.'

'A month or two! Who's going to do your job while you're swanning off somewhere?'

'You are. And you'll love it. Just as you always do.' I get to my feet even though my legs feel shaky. I am determined to have my way. 'I'm not really asking, Dad. I've made up my mind. You're right about me being a McBriar. I want this and you're going to let me have it. It's my life and I'm thirty-four-years old and financially independent. I don't need your permission. This was simply a courtesy. I'm allowed eight weeks holiday in my contract, remember. I know that because I wrote it. I'm taking them all at once. You could possibly find some reason to fire me, but you won't. So let's both agree this is for the best and I'll see you in October.' I turn to leave.

'Geneva!'

Sucking in a breath, I face him. 'Yes, Dad.'

'I wish you'd been a boy.'

'I know you do.'

'But you're one hell of a girl.' There's a flicker of pride in his eyes and the faintest hint of a smile on his mouth. 'Take your break and sort yourself out. But when you return, I don't want to hear any more of this heartbreak nonsense. And I never want to hear the name Mackenzie Fisher again. Understood?'

'Understood. Thanks, Dad.'

'Where will you go?'

I shrug as if I haven't decided. If I tell him, he might change his mind and this will turn into an all-out war.

'I'm not sure. I'll send you a text when I

get there.'

'You can use the company jet.' He picks up some papers from his desk.

'I'd planned to.'

His eyes dart back to me for a second. 'Humph! You had, had you? Get out of here, girl, before I change my mind. Some of us have work to do.'

'Thanks, Dad. Bye!'

He dismissively waves one hand in the air, returning his attention to things he considers far more important than me.

Two

I wish Dad hadn't mentioned Mack because now I can't stop thinking about him. Although, to be fair, I was thinking about Mack even before Dad spoke his name. It's all I ever think about, especially these days.

The man who broke my heart by falling in love with someone else. The man I'm still hoping I might be able to win back.

Ha! The chances of that happening are slim to say the least. Slim to none, if fact. I know that. I've seen him with his new girlfriend. He never looked at me the way he looks at her.

Until I met Mackenzie Fisher, work was the most important thing in my life and, like Dad, I was always working. The night I met Mack was a rare night out with friends.

I say friends but they're merely people I know. People I met at boarding school, or university. We stay in touch, and occasionally meet up for drinks or dinner, but we're not friends in the true sense of the word. I don't have any of those. These were simply people who, like me, have super-rich parents, and lots of money. I considered Mack a friend. Now I don't.

Mack and I met in a bar, and fell into bed together less than an hour later. It was only meant to be a one-night hook up; no surnames, no details, no phone numbers, no information about one another. But the next day, we were as astonished as each other when Mack turned up to start a new job, which happened to be at McBriar Properties. And I was Mack's new boss.

We agreed we wouldn't get involved, but the physical attraction between us was so strong we both knew it wouldn't be long until we succumbed again. We decided we'd keep things simple and uncomplicated. This was simply sex and nothing else. That suited me at the start. We were together because it was easy and it was fun. We were good together, both at work and at play.

Sadly, somewhere along the way I forgot the rules, and fell in love. I'd never been in love, so at first I didn't recognise the feeling. The closest thing I'd felt to that before was when I was a child. I had a paid nanny and I loved her very much. It was a different kind of love I felt for Nanny Tracy, of course, but that one also broke my heart.

When I did realise I loved Mack, I kept it to myself. I couldn't tell him how I felt unless he felt the same. And I knew he didn't. I'd have to get him to fall in love with me.

I know now that Mack was never going to do that. Even when I persuaded him, after we'd been 'together' for four and a half years, that we should pretend to get engaged because Dad had found out about us and he didn't want his daughter dating an employee unless it was serious.

That wasn't totally true. Dad had known about us from day one.

'You can screw whomever you want, Geneva,' he'd said, 'providing it doesn't have repercussions for this business. If I think it does, he'll go. Am I clear?'

'Completely.'

I didn't really care at the time. And at least Mack hadn't had to face 'the inquisition'. Dad already knew everything he needed to know about Mack. Or at least he thought he did. It turned out neither Dad, nor I, knew Mackenzie Fisher very well.

Sneaking around was half the fun in Mack's opinion, so I never told him Dad knew about us, until I realised I was in love. Dad had never shown Mack any indication that he knew about our relationship, so when I lied about Dad's comment, Mack had no idea it wasn't true. Mack would do anything to keep his job, so I suggested the fake engagement in the hope that, one day, he might return my feelings. I knew he would go along with it, especially after the lie about what Dad had 'said'. Mack was ambitious and he couldn't see any harm in it if it meant we could continue having fun.

But Mack didn't love me. He never said he did. And I never told him I loved him, because that would have given him the upper hand, and there was no way I could allow him to have that.

We agreed the engagement wouldn't be forever – even though I hoped our relationship would be – and that if either one of us wanted out we could say so, with no hard feelings. When I realised I was losing him, I pretended I would set him free, except I never wanted out, and I did have hard feelings.

The moment Mack met Tori, I was history, and so was our fake engagement, and nothing I could do or say, changed that.

It all happened so fast and I still can't quite believe it. I tried to get him to change his mind, but when I saw them together, I knew I had lost. I did consider revenge, and for a brief period, I tried that, but that's another story, and one of which I'm not particularly proud.

One of Tori's friends – a woman called Emma Barr – made me 'see the light', and my epiphany came as a bit of a shock.

Emma gave me a piece of her mind, and a lecture, things that no one, other than Dad and for totally different reasons, had ever done to me before. Her words had an instant impact, and caused me sleepless nights. I think Mack breaking my heart had made me vulnerable. Seeing him with Tori had made me question why he loved her right from the start, and yet, after being with me for five years, he had never felt like that about me. So Emma's lecture made me take a good, hard look at myself and my life, and I didn't like what I saw. I was as controlling as my bullying father and as selfish as my petulant mother, and something needed to change.

I've given it a lot of thought and Emma Barr was right. The thing that needs to change – is me. *I* need to change.

That's why I need this break. I feel as if the ground has given way beneath me and I'm unsure of who I am and what I want. I've never felt this way before and I don't know what to do.

At least I didn't. Until I spoke to Nanny Tracy.

I haven't told Dad that I paid a private investigator to find her, and I'm definitely not telling him that I'm going to go and stay with her. Dad thinks I'll be jetting off to somewhere exotic and staying in an exclusive resort, no doubt, like the one I often go to in Fiji. He has no idea that I'll only be taking the company jet as far as Stansted. From there I'll be taking a train, an ordinary train, to a town on the Kent coast, called Folkestone. An island ferry will take me from the Harbour Arm to the tiny island of Locke Isle, about two miles or so away, in the English Channel. Nanny Tracy and her husband, Roger will meet me at the dock and I'll be staying with them in their whitewashed cottage by the sea.

Nanny Tracy was surprised when I phoned her and even more so when I told her why. But when I asked if we could meet, she said we could do better than that.

'If you're serious about needing a break, and a complete change, why don't you come and stay with me? I'm married now, and have been for the last twenty years, to a lovely man called Roger. He knows about you because, believe it or not, I've never forgotten my little Geneva and I often wonder how you're doing. I read anything I can in the papers, but we're all aware they don't always know the truth. It would be such a joy to see you again. Of course it won't be like anything you're used to, but I can offer you a comfortable bed, a lovely view, with fresh sea air, and wholesome home cooking, plus a friendly ear and a comforting hug whenever you need one. What do you say? I think it's time to escape your golden chains and find what really matters. And what really matters, Geneva, is love.'

I almost laughed at that part and I would have, if it hadn't hurt so much. But the rest of it sounded wonderful. Especially the friendly ear, the comforting hugs, and the home cooked food. Those three things I'd only ever had from Nanny Tracy, and then recently, from Mack; I'd never had them from my parents.

'Love and I don't see eye to eye, Nanny,' I had said. 'I've just been dumped by the only man I've ever loved. And the worst part is, he never, ever loved me. But someone gave me some unsolicited advice recently. Good advice, I think, and I do need to change. I'm too much like my parents, and you and I both know that's not good. I want people to see beyond the money, beauty, glitz, and glamour. I want to be someone who has friends. Real friends. And someone who cares about others. I think you can help me do that. You can help me be the woman I genuinely want to be. Because you're the only person who has ever, truly loved me. So if you mean everything you've just said, and if you're sure your husband won't mind, I'd love to take you up on that offer. Oh, and congratulations on your marriage! I should've said that first, shouldn't I? I've got a long way to go to be a better person.'

'Nonsense! You were a wonderful child. Kind and thoughtful. Good-hearted and loving. You could be an equally wonderful adult. But it may take a little time and love. And that is something we have here, in abundance. Come as soon as you like. If you've got a pen, I'll give you all the details.'

I already had her address, thanks to the private investigator, but I wrote down details of how to get to the Harbour Arm from the train station, and where to wait for the ferry to Locke Isle.

'If the weather is too bad the ferry won't operate but thankfully those days are few and far between,' Nanny Tracy informed me. 'There is a timetable, of sorts, but give me a call when you arrive at the Harbour Arm, and I'm sure I can persuade Ward to make a special trip.'

'Ward?'

'Ward Locke. He owns and operates the ferry.'

'Ward Locke? Isn't Locke the name of the island? Does he own that too?'

'His ancestors owned everything for centuries. But since the second World War, most of the buildings and the land they're on have been sold to the residents. Ward's great grandfather was a firm believer in each man owning his own home whenever possible. He was a forward-thinker. Ward's father was the same, as is Ward. There are bits of land here and there still retained by him, and of course, he owns Locke Keep. But I'll tell you all about the island when you get here. I can't wait to give you a hug.'

'Same here. It's been far too long. I'm so, so sorry I haven't been in touch before now.'

'Don't give that a second thought. As your father said, "It would take a very brave person, or a fool", to disobey him. You were never a fool, Geneva, but I always knew that one day, you would be very brave. Now you take care. And call me from the Harbour Arm, remember.'

'I'll call you as soon as I arrive.' I rang off and sighed as a feeling of warmth spread over me.

Nanny Tracy had looked after me from the day I was born until the day Dad sent me away, in tears, to Boarding School, aged eight. I was getting, "too soft" he said, and that was due to Nanny Tracy coddling me, in his opinion. He fired her and sent her packing, telling her not to try to contact me, and he told me I was never to speak to the woman again. At eight, I was not going to disobey him, nor disregard his warning, and neither was Nanny Tracy, if she ever wanted to work again.

Nanny Tracy was the only person who had ever shown me love. Mum and Dad do love me, I think, in their own way, but they never show it and certainly never say it. And everyone knows Dad wanted a boy and was disappointed he got me. I tried hard to get Mum and Dad to show me they cared, but by the time I was sent away, I knew that was a battle I would never win. The only way I could get Dad's attention was to be more like him, so I dried my tears and built myself a shell. I would keep my emotions hidden and I would push my memories of Nanny Tracy to the back of my mind, and make Dad proud of me. That, at least, I have achieved.

But Emma Barr's words smashed through that shell. I had threatened to make her life hell, along with her friends and her family's lives, but instead of cowering and agreeing to my demands, she stood her ground and told me what she thought of me.

'Perhaps, instead of wasting your time and energy, along with everyone else's, just to seek revenge, you might be better off taking a good hard look at yourself and your life,' she said. 'Do you have friends and family who love you? Really love you. Who will do anything for you, no matter what. I somehow doubt it. Believe me, Geneva, all the money in the world won't buy you that. I mean this in a good way, be nicer, Geneva. Be better than this. You're an incredibly beautiful woman on the outside. Don't you want to be beautiful on the inside too? Wouldn't you rather people smile when they think of you, than shake with fear and loathing at the mention of your name?'

I was lost for words. I knew I was beautiful on the outside, thanks to my supermodel mother and a father with movie star good looks, but I had never considered looking on the inside.

And she wasn't finished.

'Mack loves Tori, and I'll tell you why. She is lovely and she cares about other people. Something you might want to try. It might make you feel better and happier than seeking revenge ever will. I think this is all about the fact that Mack didn't love you, and that he left you without a second thought. Let me give you some free advice. Stop trying to hurt people to get what you want, and try being nice to them for a change. You'll find you attract more bees with honey than with vinegar.'

And then, as she turned to walk away, she wished me well, and wished me happiness and love. That almost blew my mind and I was left completely speechless.

But I had my epiphany. And, as

ludicrous as it sounds, I'm glad I met Emma Barr. I called her office to thank her, but she wasn't there at the time, so I left her a message instead. I wanted her to know that what she said had hit home and that I intended to act upon it. Until that day, I would never have made a phone call like that. I would never have told someone they might have changed my life. I would never have given anyone the upper hand. Yet oddly, it felt good.

I want to feel like that every day, or at least as often as possible. And with Nanny Tracy's help, I really think I can.

Three

I board the company jet at Edinburgh early on Friday morning, to ensure I arrive at London Stansted with plenty of time for my onward travel, although I don't tell the flight crew details of the remainder of my trip. I know Dad will get his secretary to ask, and it is better for everyone if they can honestly report they have no idea of my plans. In reality, I am not entirely certain of my plans, myself.

A helicopter or a limo would be the usual mode of transport Dad and I would take from Stansted to wherever, and I could have booked either to take me directly to Folkestone. The idea did occur to me, but as part of the 'new me', and because I am seeing this entire journey as an adventure, I had decided it might be fun to use public transport, at least for part of my trip.

Searches for onward travel quickly

disabused me of that notion, but I eventually achieved a compromise. A limo would take me from Stansted airport to St Pancras station and from there, I would be catching a train to Folkestone Central.

All goes well until my arrival at St Pancras. The chauffeur escorts me inside and then I am left to my own devices. I have travelled the world since I was born, but conveying my own luggage from one point to another, is a novel experience for me, and one I must confess, I'm in no hurry to repeat.

I find the platform for the Folkestone train, but the train has not yet arrived. When it does, I forget for a second that this is public transport and I glance around for a porter or other member of staff to help me with my luggage. Then I remember that I must carry my own bags. Fortunately, a charming, fellow passenger asks if he might be of assistance.

I don't wish to brag, but men approach me all the time. Thanks to my supermodel mum and a dad with movie star good-looks, I'm a stunning brunette with waist-length, glossy hair, and long, shapely, perfectly tanned legs. My blue eyes are like sapphires (or so I am frequently told) and I have full, cherubic lips that are always bright red – apart from today. Today they're a dark cerise to match my sandals and my handbag. I often wear the tightest, shortest, sexiest clothes that leave little to the imagination, because I know the effect that has on men, and Mum taught me from an early age that if you've got it, flaunt it. But when I'm working, I wear a suit. Today my yellow strappy sundress isn't quite as short, nor as tight, but my general appearance still seems to be working its magic on this man.

I thank him profusely and he lingers for a while, but he doesn't have a first-class ticket, so he eventually moves to another compartment. Although I have to say, if this is what the owners of the train company consider 'first-class', their understanding of the term differs substantially from mine.

I begin to wish I'd taken the limo or a helicopter, especially when it begins to rain, grows heavier with each passing mile, and reaches biblical proportions within fifteen minutes of leaving the station.

An announcement over the tannoy declares that the journey may be delayed due to severe weather conditions. That doesn't bode well for my ferry trip to Locke Isle. Nanny Tracy had said the ferry sailing was weather-dependent. Trust me to pick one of the few days of atrocious weather. This is more like November than late August.

At least the WiFi connection seems to be working, as I search the internet for hotels in, or near, Folkestone. At times, when I glance out of the window, I wonder if we'll make it. I'm surprised the tracks aren't washed away in places. I phone a few hotels, with no success. Some are fully booked; others keep me on hold for so long that I end the call. Why do they play such dreadful music? Do they want people to hang up?

I am both relieved and apprehensive when the train slows on its approach to Folkestone Central, ten minutes later than the scheduled time of 1.01 p.m. which is surprisingly good, considering the torrential rain that fell throughout my journey. Miraculously, the moment the train stops, the clouds depart and the sun appears.

A fellow first-class passenger helps me with my luggage, although this man isn't quite as charming as the earlier good Samaritan. He asks if I would like to join him for a drink, and then he is annoyed when I politely turn him down. I'm tempted to let 'the old' Geneva out, and tell him precisely what I think of men like him. I decide he isn't worth it, and simply ignore him. But I run over his foot with the wheels of my suitcase, just because I can.

I exit the station and find a taxi. The driver, who I would say is in his fifties, peers at me over the rim of his sunglasses and looks me up and down, but his gaze is appreciative, not lecherous. He takes my suitcase and holdall and loads them into the boot while I stand in the sunshine and soak up the warmth.

Little plumes of vapour rise from the tarmac as the roads and pavements begin to dry out before my eyes. Perhaps I won't need to spend tonight in Folkestone after all. It's only 1.20 p.m. and if the weather continues to improve, the ferry to Locke Isle might sail.

'Where to, love?' the driver asks.

I would usually make a facetious remark to a stranger who calls me 'love', but I remind myself I'm changing my ways (despite my earlier slip when I ran over that man's foot) and I smile at him instead. At least he's holding the rear passenger door open for me. That's something. I didn't think taxi drivers did that. Our company chauffeur does, of course, and the limo driver did, naturally, but on the few occasions when I've had to resort to other vehicles for transport, the experiences have been less than satisfactory.

Today hasn't been bad though. The train journey wasn't unpleasant, all things considered, and this man seems friendly and polite, ignoring the fact he called me 'love'. I hope the ferry crossing won't be a disappointment.

'The Harbour Arm, please,' I say.

The back seat is worn but it is leather

and it's clean. I settle back and click the seatbelt into place then scroll on my phone to see the weather forecast. Sunshine and highs of twenty-three degrees. That's more like it.

'Staying in Folkestone?' the driver asks as he clicks in his own seatbelt.

'No. I'm visiting ... a family friend on Locke Isle.' Visiting my former nanny would sound somewhat pretentious.

'Beautiful place. First time?' He glances left and right, indicates and pulls away.

'Yes. First time in Folkestone, too.'

'You don't know what you've been missing. I've lived here all my life and I love the place. Mind you, it was a bit rough down by the harbour until the regeneration works began.'

'I think I read a bit about that on the internet,' I say.

'It's cost millions. And it's still ongoing. There's been extensive restoration and renovation, not just to the Harbour Arm, but the entire harbour area. The Harbour Arm itself was made from poured concrete and faced with granite and that's taken a battering over the last hundred years. It fell into disuse around 2001 and needed some intensive repair work to bring it up to scratch.'

'I read that it reopened to the public as a pier in 2015.'

He nods. 'There were only a handful of food outlets at first. Since then, local businesses have sprung up in The Goods Yard, the Marketplace, and on the Harbour Arm. From gourmet coffee shops to fish and chips. Some of the businesses are housed in the old, revamped station buildings, some in shipping containers, and some are pop-ups. There's even a big, blue bus. It's called The Big Greek Bus, and if you like Greek food, you'll love that.'

'I do like Greek food. Very much. But I've never eaten food served from a bus. I'll look out for it.' I don't add, to avoid it. And perhaps I shouldn't pre-judge. The food might be delicious even if the surroundings aren't quite up to my usual expectations.

'You'll find places serving Mexican, Argentinian, and Thai food, too,' he says. 'Plus there's freshly baked bread, ice-cream and waffles, pizzas, hot-dogs, burgers, ribs, fish and chips as I said, and, if you have a more refined palate, which I suspect you might by the look of you, there's lobster, mussels, oysters and more.'

'I look like I have a refined palate?' I'm a little surprised. I took great pains to look like everyone else. At least I thought I had.

He grins at me via the rear-view mirror. 'As my old mum always says, "If you're a true Princess, wearing a rubbish bag won't hide that, but if you're trash, wearing a tiara won't make you a princess." Probably shouldn't say stuff like that, but she's right.'

'I'm not a princess.' I'm not sure if I should be flattered or annoyed. I've been called a princess before, sometimes as a form of endearment and sometimes not.

'I meant that in a good way,' he says, the look of concern apparent as his eyes dart to the mirror once again.

I relax and smile. 'Thanks.'

He coughs to clear his throat and continues. 'There're a few bars, a microbrewery and, you might be pleased to hear, a Champagne bar. That's housed in the renovated lighthouse right at the end of the Arm and it has one of the best views around. Plus, the lighthouse still functions. On a clear day you can see France, but on most days you can see Locke Isle, and of course, the sea.' He grins. 'If you look to shore from there, you'll see miles of coastline and the famous White Cliffs, plus the fishing harbour. There's often live music and bands, but due to this morning's weather, a few places may be shut, and you might not get to see the area at its best today.'

'It sounds wonderful.' It has also made me long for a glass of champagne, but I won't mention that after the princess comment. I scroll on my phone to find details of the opening hours.

'Not boring you am I, love?'

I look up from my phone and meet his eyes in the mirror. 'No. I was just googling the Harbour Arm.'

'Checking up to see if I'm telling the truth?' His grin is still friendly.

'No. I believe you. I was merely searching for additional information. Your comments about all the amazing food have made me feel hungry and I'm thinking I should eat here before I make the crossing to Locke Isle. I don't want to arrive at Nan...new surroundings and immediately ask for food.'

'I can tell you everything you want to know.'

I slip my phone back into my handbag, and smile. 'Tell me more.'

'About the food, or the Harbour Arm? Are you interested in history?'

'Both. And yes I am.'

'Great. I know plenty. I'd recommend The Lighthouse Tasting Rooms for lunch. That's in the old station buildings and it's run by the same team as The Lighthouse Champagne Bar. You'll feel right at home, and the food is delicious. Everything is good there.'

I didn't ask what he meant by me feeling right at home.

'Now for the history. Stop me if you get

bored. I'll keep it brief. It's been a trading port since Roman times, some say even before. Boats have fished from here since the 1100s and there's been a proper fishing fleet here for centuries. The stone harbour was constructed in stages between about 1807 and 1830, but the owners went broke. Prior to that it was wooden jetties. The South Eastern Railway Company purchased it in 1843 and built the Harbour branch line and a viaduct, and freight trains ran here from 1844. The first passenger train arrived in early 1849. You could get a train from London right to the station on the harbour, and from there a steam packet would take you to Boulogne and then another train would get you to Paris. Now Eurostar does the journey in a fraction of the time. Or there's *LeShuttle*, as it's now known. That will take you and your car from the Eurotunnel terminal up the road, to Calais in thirty-five minutes. Not as romantic though, eh?'

'Eurostar can be romantic.'

'First class, maybe.' He grins at me again. 'Anyway, back to the history lesson. That new pier was called 'Horn Pier'. It jutted out into deeper water so larger ships could dock. It was extended during the late 1890s and early 1900s, and it's now the Harbour Arm. In the first World War, troops and mail were sent from there, to and from the Western Front, and during the Dunkerque evacuation in 1940, every boat in Folkestone brought troops back to waiting trains at the harbour station. Ferry sailings resumed to Boulogne after WWII, but the harbour is relatively shallow and what with competition from the Dover to Calais route and then the Channel Tunnel, its days were numbered. Services stopped in 2001 and the area went downhill, but the railway station and branch line weren't officially closed by the Department for Transport until around 2014.'

'That's rather sad, given its long history.'

'Yeah. Most of the rails that ran to the end of the Harbour Arm were taken up, but the station buildings house the bars and food outlets I mentioned, so it isn't all bad. The station itself and ferry terminal have been adapted and restored, so they haven't been completely lost. You'll see all this yourself, because here we are. Folkestone Harbour, in all its glory.'

'Gosh. That was quick.'

I've been listening so intently that I haven't noticed anything on the way here, and now I'm a little annoyed with myself for not looking out of the window.

The driver smiles at me via the mirror. 'The traffic was lighter than usual. I expect

33

folks are thinking it might pour down again so they're staying indoors.' He gets out, opens the door for me, and goes to the boot to retrieve my luggage. 'I didn't even have time to tell you about Locke Isle.' He smiles again and points towards the sea. 'There it is. Enjoy your lunch, and have a lovely time on the island.'

'Thanks,' I say, as I see Locke Isle for the first time. 'It's closer than I expected. And smaller.'

'Yep. That's what everyone says. I think most people imagine it's the size of the Isle of Wight, down Hampshire way, but it's about a sixth of that. The Isle of Wight is around twenty-three miles by thirteen miles. Locke Isle is a little over four miles long and two and a half miles wide. But there's still plenty to see and lots of things to do there.'

I can't imagine what, but I'll take his word for it.

After paying the fare, giving a generous tip, and thanking him for such an enjoyable journey, I stand and stare at the island for a moment. I can make out a lighthouse at one end and a church at the other and smack-bang in the centre, Locke Keep stands proud, a flag flying from a tower. I assume the Keep is square and has four towers, but from here I can only see three. At a quick guess I would say there are about forty or so houses on this side of the island and I wonder if the other side mirrors it. They all have colourful facades beneath red roofs and they sit on the hill, and appear to surround Locke Keep. I can see a few trees and what I think may be a couple of roads, one road leading down to the white cliffs and the beach below. I can also see a row of buildings raised up from the beach and what appears to be some sort of jetty or wooden pier. If that boat moored up beside it is the ferry, it is also much smaller than I had imagined.

Perhaps the island is larger than it looks and it stretches out behind the Keep, with many more houses, a shopping centre, restaurants, and considerably more than I can see from here. Something inside me tells me not to hold out much hope. Four miles by two and a half miles is not very big.

But then again, it is larger than each of the islands in The Maldives, and I've had a lot of fun on a few of those over the years. Although the weather, sea and sand of an island in the English Channel will bear no comparison to that of the Indian Ocean.

Four

I make my way towards the Harbour Arm, avoiding puddles the size of small ponds and tip-toeing between some cobbles, in my high-heeled sandals.

I really should've given more thought to my attire. My thin-strapped, sunshine-yellow sundress would've been drenched if the rain hadn't stopped. I hadn't thought to pack a raincoat, and I'd left my showerproof jacket in my hall cupboard. I meant to grab that on my way out, but a phone call from Dad had distracted me as I was dashing out of my apartment.

'I hear you're only taking the jet as far as Stansted,' Dad said. 'Have you booked alternative travel from there? Your secretary doesn't seem to have a clue. I gave you permission to use it, girl. So use it.'

'No need to worry, Dad. I don't need the jet, thanks. Someone is meeting me,' I lied. It wasn't a total lie though. Nanny Tracy and Roger are meeting me ... on Locke Isle. 'I've got to dash,' I added, 'but I'll text you later.' The chauffeur driving one of the company limos from my apartment to the airport would wait, as would the pilot of the company jet, but I'd booked a limo from Stansted to St Pancras, and although that would also wait, if I requested it, I wanted to give myself plenty of time for my onward travel. 'Look after yourself while I'm away.'

'Look after...? Geneva? What are you playing at?'

'Nothing, Dad. Everything is fine,' I reassured him.

But not everything was fine. Thanks to his call, I'd forgotten my showerproof jacket and I hadn't realised that until it began to rain.

Perhaps I should buy one now, in Folkestone. I'm sure there must be a few shops on Locke Isle, even if there isn't a shopping centre, but Folkestone will have a better selection.

My tummy rumbles and I remember all the wonderful places the taxi driver mentioned. Waterproof clothing can wait. I'd had coffee, and a bowl of cereal at 6.00 a.m. at my apartment, and I'd had more coffee, and a croissant with butter and raspberry jam, just the way I like it, on the jet, but I am nervous about seeing Nanny Tracy after all these years – and when I'm nervous, I get hungry.

The aroma of freshly baked bread wafts towards me as I enter the area known as The Goods Yard. This is where several of those pop-up eateries are situated and as I stroll along towards the Harbour Arm itself which juts out before me into the English Channel like an arm bent at the elbow, my senses are overloaded with an abundance of aromas, sights and sounds and I don't know where to look. Some places are clearly reopening after this morning's dreadful weather and I'm surrounded by people as the place buzzes with activity.

I see the Marketplace where local traders and craftspeople sell their wares, and as I continue on my way, I search for the wide slipway at the end of the Harbour Arm car park where Nanny Tracy told me the ferry from Locke Isle will dock.

The slipway looks small, but then the ferry isn't large. Nanny Tracy told me it only has enough space on its main deck to accommodate four cars, and seating for a maximum of twenty people on its upper deck, part of which is enclosed, and part of which is not. Vehicular access to the island is restricted and only residents of the island, or those who are issued passes, are permitted to take their vehicles on the ferry.

I glance at my watch to check the time. I want to see how long it takes me to walk from here to The Lighthouse Tasting Rooms. I plan to have something delicious there for lunch, so I want to be sure how long it will take me to return to the car park and then add extra time to walk to the slipway to meet the ferry. But before I eat lunch, I intend to continue on to the lighthouse itself, where I shall sit and admire the view, and have at least one glass of champagne at The Lighthouse Champagne Bar. I can't imagine Nanny Tracy and Roger will have much champagne, if any, at their cottage, and this might be my last chance to enjoy a glass or two of my favourite tipple.

The problem is, I'm already enjoying the view so much that I forget to check my watch when I stop to read the menu at The Lighthouse Tasting Rooms, or to look at it again when I take a seat at The Lighthouse Champagne Bar. It isn't until I'm halfway through my first glass of champagne that I remember.

I'm sure it was only a matter of minutes. Ten or possibly fifteen at most. I'll have another glass, and then I'll have some lunch. After that I'll call Nanny Tracy and let her know I'm here. That should be around 3.00 p.m. or so.

She said she would ask Ward Locke to make a special trip to meet me, if I arrive outside of the schedule, but the schedule changes if the weather is bad, so after all the rain, I have no idea what it is.

In any event I'm sure I'll have plenty of time to make it back to the slipway to meet the ferry, although I do want to stop off at the Marketplace and buy some flowers, and a gift or two. I can't arrive empty-handed, especially after all these years. Nanny Tracy and Roger are doing me a massive favour by letting me stay with them, and although, of course, I'll offer to pay for my stay, I still need to arrive with some gifts. But I can worry about that later.

I order a second glass, and bask in the sunshine as the warmth makes me relax. I could close my eyes and drift off, sitting here. But obviously I must not do that. Perhaps a second glass of bubbly wasn't such a good idea.

I pay the bill and make my way back along the Harbour Arm to the restaurant, where I order half a dozen Rock Oysters, followed by King Prawn and Scallop Orzo, and I can't resist the Tarte au Chocolat for dessert, all washed down with two more glasses of champagne. I'm convinced the island won't have a restaurant like this and I might not be able to nip back here via the ferry, if the weather turns again, so I may as well make the most of my time here.

I won't be shopping for a waterproof jacket after this, so I hope it doesn't rain. If I can't buy one on the island, perhaps Nanny Tracy will have a spare one I can borrow. I realise I haven't called her yet, and when I check my watch, it is 3.15 p.m. so I had better get a move on. The bill is very reasonable. I'll definitely come here again.

I call Nanny Tracy and explain I lost track of time. She tells me not to worry and says she'll speak to Ward and call me back. A few minutes later she informs me that Ward will meet me at the ferry dock in half an hour and she reminds me where the slipway is. When I ask if I need to buy a ticket from somewhere here or if I pay as I board, she chuckles.

'No need to worry about that,' she says. 'It's all taken care of.'

I seem to be having trouble walking now and it takes me longer than I expected to return to the Marketplace. I buy a beautiful bouquet of red roses from a pop-up florist, because I remember they were Nanny Tracy's favourite flower, and I buy Roger a box of handmade chocolates because I have no idea what he likes, but everyone likes chocolate. I also buy some heavenly-scented soaps, an ornately crafted candle, two watercolours of the Harbour Arm, one as it was in its heyday of steam packets to France, and one as it is now. Maybe I'll give those to Roger and keep the chocolates for myself. No. I'll give the chocolates to Nanny Tracy and Roger in addition to the watercolours.

I see so many things I could buy but I can't carry much more and besides, I mustn't be late for the ferry, so I walk towards the slipway and stand on the cobbled edge, staring out towards Locke Isle.

The ferry still looks tiny from here, but with each passing second it grows larger. It takes about ten minutes to cover the stretch of sea but another three or four to position itself for approach and a further four or so to manoeuvre the metal gangway into position, although that is done by machine.

I stand well out of the way and wait for the two vehicles on the main deck to drive off but the warm breeze wafts car exhaust and ferry diesel fumes directly at me. I gag as I inhale the toxic cloud that also makes my stomach lurch. I've only sailed on superyachts and luxury cruise liners and they are a far cry from this. I'm now having concerns about the final leg of my trip and I shut my eyes tight behind my sunglasses, in the hope I won't be sick. Swimming to the island might be preferable.

A high-pitched and exceedingly youthful

voice asks, 'Are you the lady visiting Nanny Tracy?' and when I open my eyes, a small girl with rich, auburn curls, dimples, and the greenest eyes I've ever seen, is standing right in front of me, beaming up at me. 'I'm the ferry captain.'

My brows shoot up. She can't be serious. And then it dawns on me that this child just called my former nanny, Nanny Tracy. I wonder why.

A burst of deep laughter draws my attention to the tall man walking towards us. He has similar hair to the girl, but his is more wavy than curly, and much shorter than hers. He's in his mid to late thirties, I would guess and I can't help but notice he's not only fit, he's handsome. With his sunglasses pushed up on to the top of his head, he's eyeing me as intently as I am him, although luckily for me, my sunglasses hide the fact I'm ogling him. He has the same green eyes as the girl, but there's an extra something in his. I take in the black T-shirt, faded jeans, and the metal-toe-caps on his well-worn, leather boots and wonder who he is. This can't possibly be Ward Locke, the man who owns the ferry, Locke Keep, and the island – or some of it.

'I'm the third mate,' he says, in a voice as delicious and as smooth as the finest milk chocolate. And then a black Labrador comes bounding forward. 'He's the second mate. Our first mate isn't currently with us. And you must be ... Sorry. Tracy did tell me, but I've forgotten your name.'

'Oh. It's Gen,' I say, acknowledging the man has a sense of humour. 'With a 'G'.'

I have told Nanny Tracy that, if possible, I want to keep things simple and try to be incognito. I know that might be a big ask, given that I am who I am, but not everyone knows the name Geneva McBriar, or McBriar Properties, and even if they do, I can pretend I simply look like her. I'm not trying to deceive anyone. I just don't want Dad to find out where I am. Or the paparazzi.

'Hello, Gen with a G. This is my daughter, Eve. This is Horatio, our dog. And I'm Ward.'

A gasp escapes me, but I quickly turn it into a cough. 'Pleased to meet you,' I manage. 'Sorry. The fumes are making me cough. Does the ferry always smell like this?'

His dark brows furrow as if he doesn't understand the question. 'It's a ferry. Here, let me help you with your bags. The wind is picking up. We should make a move. More rain is on the way and the weather can change in a matter of seconds around here.'

He takes my suitcase, holdall, and my shopping bags, but not the flowers, leaving me with one hand free which, to my astonishment, Eve takes in hers and leads me on to the metal gangway.

'Careful,' she says. 'This can be slippy.'

'Slippery, you mean?'

'No.' She shakes her head and mimics the furrowed brows of her father. 'Slippy. It's a word. It's in the dictionary.'

Wonderful. I'm getting English lessons from a precocious child.

'I know it is. But slippery sounds better.'

'No it doesn't. I like slippy.'

To add insult to injury – or injury to insult in this case – I promptly slip. I almost pull the child over as my arms flail in the air. The flowers I'm holding go flying, but her grip on my other hand is vice-like. I manage to grab the pop-up, chain railings on the gangway and somehow steady myself, although I seem to be swaying slightly.

'See,' Eve says, and I'm sure that's a grin on her face. 'It's slippy.'

'Are you okay?' Ward looks concerned, but I think he's grinning too. I'm so glad they both find this amusing.

'Yes,' I snap, and then I search around me for the roses.

'They've gone overboard, I'm afraid.' Ward nods his head sideways as he deposits my luggage and shopping bags against a circular pillar on the main deck; a pillar about three feet tall and at least two feet in

45

circumference, clearly metal beneath the white paint.

He grabs a long pole from some hooks on the inside hull of the ferry, and returns to where I'm standing.

I teeter a little closer to the edge, still gripping the chain railings with one hand, the other remaining tightly in Eve's grasp, as we all peer over the side, including Horatio, the dog, and Ward hooks the bedraggled flowers from the water.

'I think they're okay,' he says, holding the dripping bouquet towards me. Horatio barks as if he agrees.

'Thanks.' There is no way I am taking those from him. 'Is there any chance I could go and buy some more? I don't want to turn up empty-handed and roses are N...Tracy's favourite flowers.'

Again his brows meet. 'What's wrong with these?' He's still holding them out towards me.

I raise my brows in reply, let go of the chain railings, and lift my sunglasses momentarily with my forefinger and thumb. 'Apart from the fact they are covered in both salt water, and no doubt, diesel oil, you mean?'

He shrugs. 'They look fine.'

'They're not. Please take my word for that.'

His eyes meet mine and we stare at one another in silence. It's only a matter of seconds but something passes between us.

Ward is undeniably attractive but I've recently had my heart broken and I'm not here to have a holiday romance. Besides, he's got a child. And, I assume, also a wife.

And then it's gone, and now he looks a little annoyed.

'If we're going ashore,' Eve says enthusiastically, 'may I have an ice cream, please, Dad?'

He drags his gaze from me, glances down at her and smiles, hesitating for a moment before he answers.

'Sorry, honey. We don't have time to go ashore. Bad weather is coming, I can feel it. It may quickly pass, but best not take any chances. We don't want to be stuck here for the night, do we? We'll get ice cream from White Cliffs Café.'

'Okay, Dad,' she says, letting go of my hand and skipping on to the deck of the ferry, with Horatio following behind her.

I'm tempted to say that I would be happy to be stuck in Folkestone for the night.

'But I need flowers!' I say.

'There's a florist next door to the café, on Boardwalk, which is where the ferry docks. We need to go. Please clear the gangway.'

He seems a lot less friendly now and I

wonder what I've said or done to cause this change as I follow him on to the deck.

Is it because I wouldn't take the flowers from him?

He lays them on top of the circular pillar against which he's left the rest of my things, and strides away.

I stop at the pillar and watch him. I'm not sure what to make of him. He owns an island and lives in an ancient Keep, which although not technically a castle, resembles one, and yet he runs a ferry on which he seems perfectly at home. He looks like a man who should own a superyacht, but dresses like a man who can only stretch to the cost of a toy boat for his bath. With his good-looks he could easily be a player. Instead he is clearly a devoted Dad. And yet there was definitely a moment between us. I'm sure I didn't imagine that. But I remind myself he's married and I need to dismiss him from my thoughts. Besides, my heart is broken, and I'm here to change my ways, not have a new romance.

I glance back towards the Marketplace and consider dashing ashore, but I can already hear the engine revving, and the gangway shudders as it slowly retracts back on to the deck. I know it's ridiculous but I suddenly feel as if I'm leaving civilisation behind me and heading off to an island penal colony, or some such thing.

The ferry judders as it reverses from the slipway and my entire body shakes as we leave the quayside. I collect my things and go in search of somewhere to sit. I don't think I'm going to enjoy this trip. The smell of diesel hits me once more and I swallow several times in the hope my stomach settles.

'Come up here!' Eve yells at me from the upper deck as she leans out in a perfect diagonal from a metal and glass box-like structure that I assume is the wheelhouse. She's only holding on with one hand while she waves at me with the other. 'Leave your things down there.'

She must've seen me look at the flight of metal steps and then down at my luggage and shopping. I don't know how old she is but she seems oddly mature for a small child, and completely at home on this vessel.

I hang on to the handrail as I make my way up and I'm relieved when I reach the upper deck. Ward doesn't look at me, he's busy manoeuvring the ferry and seems to be using an old-fashioned brass and mahogany ship wheel to steer it. The wheel looks like it came from a much grander ship than this ferry boat but I don't ask for details. I don't want to interrupt his concentration. Horatio, the black Labrador, is curled up in a dog-bed just a few feet from Ward, and Eve leaps out of the wheelhouse like the child she really is, and attempts to make me jump. I pretend to be scared ... and right now, that's not difficult.

Tantalising sounds of music and laughter reach me and I gaze longingly at The Lighthouse Champagne Bar as we sail past. Oh to be back there, sipping champagne. I see a bench opposite the wheelhouse, and sit. My legs are like jelly and so is my stomach.

'Don't you like boats?' Eve asks, sitting beside me.

'Yes, and I'm a good sailor. But this is not the type of boat I'm used to. It's a ferry, and it's my first time on a boat like this.'

'I'll tell you a secret,' she says, leaning close. 'It's not really a ferry. It's a pirate ship. *My* pirate ship. But we use it as a ferry because people need to get on and off our island. Gosh. Are you going to be sick?'

I gag again and swallow hard.

'It's the fumes. Or maybe, something I ate.'

'Or you had a few too many glasses of wine on the Harbour Arm,' Ward says.

I look across at him and he tosses me a small bottle of water, which I miss. It thwacks against my arm, lands on the deck, and rolls away from me, but Eve jumps up, grabs it, and hands it to me with a smile.

'Thanks,' I say to her.

'Sorry,' says Ward. 'I thought you'd catch it.'

I give him a tight smile, unscrew the cap, and take several refreshing gulps from the water in the plastic bottle.

'Why are you here?' Ward asks.

'What? I'm visiting ... Tracy, a family friend.' That's the second time I've lied about that. Although Nanny Tracy is a friend. Or I hope she will be.

'I know who you are, Miss McBriar, although I didn't realise it until a little while ago. And I know what you do. If you've got your eye on Locke Isle, you'll have a wasted journey. It's not for sale and it never will be. And if you think a pair of sunglasses can hide your identity for long, you're mistaken.'

'Oh!' I was about to say something facetious, but I'm trying to be a better person, so instead I smile and slide my sunglasses down to the tip of my nose. 'Really? It worked for *Clark Kent*. And he wore ordinary glasses.' The look of surprise is worth it and a hint of a smile tugs at the corner of his mouth. 'As for having my eye on the island, nothing could be farther from my reason for being here, I assure you. I am genuinely here to visit a friend. And her husband. I'm actually taking a break from work.'

'Taking a break? On Locke Isle? I

would've thought somewhere exotic with a luxury hotel would be more up your street.'

'It would have, normally, and to be honest, I'm wondering if this is a wise decision. But ... let's just say, I'm turning over a new leaf.'

'A new leaf?'

I nod. I'm not going to explain myself to a man I've just met.

'So Tracy and Roger are friends of yours?' He looks sceptical.

'Tracy is, yes.'

'And yet you've never been here before, even though Tracy joined Roger on Locke Isle twenty years ago, and you didn't attend the wedding. I would remember if you had.'

I cough while I think of a response. I'm feeling queasy again and I wish he would shut up.

'Unfortunately, due to other commitments, I couldn't make it to the wedding. And, as you said, my holidays are usually somewhere exotic with a luxury hotel. I don't take many holidays, it may surprise you to know, and until this extended break I'm having now, our schedules have clashed.'

'Schedules?' he queries, but I don't answer.

'Are you rich?' Eve asks.

I nod again. This time because bile is

creeping up my throat and I'm afraid to speak. The ferry is rolling and the sea isn't as calm as it was when we left the harbour.

'Money doesn't buy happiness, honey,' Ward says to his daughter.

'But it can buy a lot of ice cream,' she replies, looking wistful. 'And chocolate milkshake. And cake.'

The ferry lurches and so does my stomach. I cover my mouth with my hand and swallow several times but there's nothing I can do to stop it. Eve dashes out of the way but Ward hurries forward with a sick bag, which thankfully, catches most of it. He sits beside me and when I stop throwing up, I realise he is holding back my hair with one hand and still holding the bag with the other.

'Grab some wet wipes, please,' he instructs Eve. 'And the mop.'

Seconds later, she hands me a wipe and then starts mopping the deck around my feet, even though the length of the mop handle is twice her height. She's obviously done this before. Luckily, I don't appear to have any vomit on me or my sandals, but I could die from embarrassment.

'Thanks,' I say, when I can speak. 'Sorry about that. Wait! Who is steering the ferry?'

Ward grins at me as he lets my hair slip gently through his fingers so that it falls down my back and doesn't flop forward into my face.

'She may look old but she does have some mod-cons.'

'Dad means the boat, not me,' Eve says, and as the ferry lurches once more, adds, 'You're not going to be sick again, are you?'

'Drink some water,' Ward commands, getting to his feet and handing me the bottle that was by my side. 'The weather's turned. I need to get back to the wheel, and you should get inside.' I'm glad he takes the sickbag with him.

He's not kidding about the weather. The sun has disappeared and the sky is now a foreboding grey with clouds the size of Locke Isle, rolling towards us from the west. We're only halfway across and the sea is getting choppy. I can't take my eyes from the sky as a curtain of rain appears in the distance and heads in our direction.

'My shopping!' I remember I've left my things on the deck below.

'I'll move them under shelter,' says Eve, leaning the mop inside the wheelhouse and dashing towards the stairs.

I realise I'm about to be drenched at any moment but I can't seem to move. I can hear Ward calling me, and then Eve pops up again, grabs my hand, and leads me to the wheelhouse, closing the door behind us. Seconds later, torrential rain slashes against the ferry like machine gun fire.

'Well isn't this cosy?' says Ward, as the ferry lurches and rolls, and Horatio yawns and stretches in his dog-bed.

The wheelhouse is big enough for the three of us, and the dog, but in the enclosed space I can smell the aftershave Ward is wearing. I hope he can smell my expensive perfume, and that I don't reek of vomit.

'Don't throw up in here,' says Eve, reading my mind and sounding more and more like a forty-year-old every time she speaks.

'I'll try not to,' I say, and then change the subject. 'I don't have a raincoat. Or even a waterproof jacket.'

'You may not need one,' Ward says.

I gasp. 'Are you suggesting we might drown! That really isn't funny.'

'No!' He bursts out laughing and points ahead. I'm standing facing towards him so I have my back to the island but when I swivel round, I see the sky before us over Locke Isle, is blue. 'I told you the weather can change around here in an instant. This is just a squall and we'll be out of it in no time.'

I hope Ward is right. I've never been so thankful to see dry land and blue sky, in my entire life.

I momentarily lose my balance and stumble sideways into him. His body is warm and solid against mine and as I use my left hand to help push myself away from him his muscles tighten beneath my fingers. He smells even better this close up and when our eyes meet briefly, all sorts of thoughts tumble around in my head. Thoughts I shouldn't be having, especially not if this man's child can read my mind. He keeps one hand on the wheel and steadies me with the other. The bare skin on my upper arm tingles at his touch, and as his lips part, I imagine what it might be like to kiss him.

'Hang on to that rail,' he says, completely ruining the moment as he nods towards a metal bar just inside the door. That must be what Eve was hanging on to as she leant out earlier.

Now I feel a fool for letting my imagination run away with me. Ward was clearly not having similar thoughts about me.

But this is the first time I have had such thoughts about any man other than Mackenzie Fisher. So maybe this isn't all bad.

Except, this man has a daughter.

And, no doubt, a wife.

Although the only ring he's wearing is a signet ring on the little finger of his left hand.

Five

'We'll be there in five minutes,' Ward says. 'Are Tracy and Roger meeting you?'

'Yes. But I'm wondering if I should call and tell them not to. I'd like to replace the flowers. The island doesn't look that big, even now we're closer, and I'm sure I can find my way to their cottage. Or you could probably tell me how to get there. You said there's a florist near to where the ferry docks?'

'Yes. On Boardwalk. That's the wooden pier and it leads round, in a raised L-shape to a parade of shops. That's where you'll find White Cliffs Café, Buds and Blooms the florist, and Locke's Convenience Store.'

'Locke's Convenience Store? Do you own that?'

'My aunt does.'

'Your aunt? That's ... convenient.'

He grins suddenly. 'It is. There are a few

other shops on Boardwalk, but most of the shops are on Main Road, which as the name suggests, is the main road on the island. There are a few more shops and businesses on Lighthouse Way, which is to the left of Boardwalk and leads to the lighthouse, and some on Church Road to the right, which leads to the church.' The grin broadens. 'We like to keep things simple on the island.'

'I don't suppose there's a clothing shop, is there?'

'You're in luck. There's one on Boardwalk and another on Main Road. But you won't find any of the designer labels that you're used to buying, in either.'

I raise my brows at that. 'How do you know what I'm used to buying?' I laugh. 'Don't judge a book by its cover. Anyway, right now it's not the label I care about. It's keeping me dry that's important.'

'Then you're definitely in luck. And I'm sorry. You're right. One should never judge a book by its cover. Oh and, yes. I can tell you how to get to White Cliffs Cottage.'

'Wait. Let me guess. It's on the white cliffs. The address is White Cliffs Cottage, 1 White Cliffs Walk, and you said the islanders like to keep things simple. Oh! But there are two white cliffs, aren't there?' I'm facing forward now and I can clearly see the two large white cliffs that were also visible from the Harbour Arm in Folkestone. They sit either side of a grassy section of cliff, and the hill, and the road that leads down to Boardwalk where the ferry docks. I can now clearly see the parade of shops he mentioned. 'You'll need to tell me which white cliff the cottage is on.'

'White Cliffs Walk is on the right, and Tracy and Roger's cottage is the yellow one, just there. That first cottage, directly above Boardwalk.'

He's pointing to a large cottage situated fairly close to the cliff edge, but thankfully not as close as an almost identical cottage opposite, on the other cliff to the left. That other cottage looks precariously close to the edge, whereas Nanny Tracy and Roger's cottage at least has a road between it and the drop to the beach. Although if their cottage fell, it looks as though it would land on whatever sits behind the parade of shops on Boardwalk.

'Is coastal erosion a serious problem on the island?' I ask. 'I'm assuming it must be.'

He turns and glances at Eve. She is now sitting on the floor stroking Horatio who is still curled up in his dog-bed.

Ward nods and lowers his voice as if he would prefer Eve not to hear. 'Yes. But the leeward side of the island isn't as bad as the windward side because this side is slightly sheltered by the mainland and the seaward side, as it's also known, takes the worst of the battering from the winds and stormy seas. We do what we can, and the government gives a small amount towards the sea defences but it's not nearly enough.'

I want to ask more but decide this is probably not the time. He didn't want Eve to hear, so it's best if I ask my questions when she is not around. Or I can ask Nanny Tracy and Roger. Although as their home is near the cliff edge, it may be a sensitive subject. I can probably find out what I need to know from the internet.

'I'll phone and tell them not to meet me then,' I say. 'But it would be good not to have to drag my luggage around the shops.' I sigh without meaning to.

'You're probably used to staff doing that for you.'

'Hey! What happened to not judging?' I can see he's grinning so I don't bother defending myself and I go along with it instead. 'Absolutely. Hundreds of them. I should've sent some on ahead. What was I thinking?'

'I have no idea. But it's so hard to get good staff these days. Which is why I'm currently running the ferry business myself. Along with Captain Eve, of course.'

'Not forgetting your second mate,

Horatio,' I add.

'Who could forget Horatio?' Ward says, grinning at me as Eve jumps to her feet at the mention of her name, and Horatio promptly barks at the mention of his.

'Don't forget you promised we could have ice cream at the café,' Eve reminds her father.

'I haven't forgotten.' He ruffles her curls with one hand and bends down and kisses the top of her head. And then he looks up and smiles. 'I have an idea.'

'Careful,' I say. 'Don't overdo it.'

He pulls a face. 'I was going to offer to look after your luggage while you shopped,' he says, 'but now...' His voice trails off as he grins at me.

'Oh! That's a brilliant idea. Do you mean it?'

'I never say anything I don't mean. We're having ice cream at the café, so as long as you don't take hours, we can do that, and you can meet us when you're done.'

'Perfect!' I pull my phone from my handbag and ring Nanny Tracy. 'I'll let them know. What time do the shops shut on the island?'

He looks as though he may be regretting his offer. 'Around 5.30 p.m., why? You won't be hours, will you?'

'It's already gone 4.00 p.m. so I can't be,

can I?' I hold a finger up to ask him to wait as Nanny Tracy answers. 'Hello! I just wanted to let you know that I'm almost at the island, but there's no need to come and meet me. I'm having a quick coffee with Ward and Eve, oh, and Horatio, if that's okay with you and Roger.'

'Oh how lovely!' she replies. 'Don't you rush on our account. We'll be here whenever you're ready.'

'Thanks, Nanny,' I say, forgetting myself, and I see the small furrow in Ward's brow. 'Um. I'll make my own way to your cottage after that.'

'Ward will help you with your luggage, I'm sure, but if you need a hand, call and let us know.'

'Thank you. Yes, Ward has already offered to carry all my luggage for me.' I grin at him and he shakes his head. 'I'll be with you by 6.00 p.m. at the latest.' Ward sighs at that. 'Bye for now.' I ring off and beam at him.

He tuts loudly. 'Remind me to keep my ideas to myself in future,' he says, but I can see his mouth is twitching and he's trying hard not to laugh.

'I'll pay for the ice cream,' I offer.

He raises his brows. 'Didn't you say you were joining us for coffee? Or was that a fib? And are you going to fill me in on the

62

"Nanny" bit?'

'I will happily join you for coffee. But I do need to shop first.'

'Why am I not surprised?' he teases. 'And the "Nanny"? Does that mean what I think it means?'

'Oh!' says Eve, as if the penny has just dropped. 'Is Nanny Tracy your nanny too? She often looks after me and that's what I call her. Did she look after you?'

'She did. From the day I was born until, oh, probably about your age. How old are you, anyway? Forty-five?'

Eve gasps and giggles. 'I'm eight. Dad's forty-five.'

'Thanks,' he says. 'I'm a mere thirty-six, but I do feel forty-five sometimes. I think today is one of those times.' He glances at me. 'I'm not sure why.'

I grin. 'I have that effect on people. It's a gift.'

'You've definitely had an effect on me, Gen, with a G. I think I'll remember this trip for months to come.'

I can't tell from his expression whether he means that in a good, or a bad, way.

I hope it's not the latter.

Six

Docking doesn't take as long this time because there are no vehicles on board so the metal gangway isn't required.

'We'll exit via a much smaller gangway on the starboard side, for foot passengers only,' Ward informs me.

'Is there anything I can do to help?' I ask, as he pulls alongside the wooden jetty. Or Boardwalk, I suppose I should call it.

He grins. 'Stay out of the way until I tell you it's okay to come down.'

'I'm the captain, remember,' Eve says.

'Yes ma'am,' I salute her and she laughs. 'Erm. Your second mate seems reluctant to perform his duties, Captain,' I add, looking at Horatio, curled up and snoring.

'Those are his duties,' says Ward, grinning as he edges past me.

I should have stepped back, but I'm ridiculously glad I didn't. His body wouldn't have brushed against me and his eyes wouldn't have locked with mine if I had – and I liked the feeling, even if it was only for a second or two.

I watch him as he hurries towards the main deck and Eve follows behind him.

What is the matter with me?

What am I doing?

I know I haven't been myself since Mack fell for Tori and left both me and McBriar Properties, and that Emma's comments made me rethink everything I thought I believed and understood, but this is getting silly.

Ward has a daughter.

Ward is a married man. At least I think he is.

Ward shouldn't matter to me. None of this should. I'm here to sort myself and my life out and to decide what I want for my future.

And that certainly isn't Ward. And Eve. And Horatio.

'It's safe,' he yells, a minute or two later.

I'm not sure it is. I'm not sure it's safe for me to be anywhere near Ward right now.

'Get a grip, Geneva,' I tell myself.

That's what Dad would say. Actually, Dad would say a lot of things if he knew where I was at this precise moment.

That thought sobers me, and brings me

back to the reality of my situation. I pull myself together, straighten my back, and make my way down to the main deck.

'I'll help you off,' Ward says. 'And then, when Eve and I have finished here, we'll take your luggage and shopping bags ashore, and we'll meet you later in White Cliffs Café. When the shops have shut.' He heaves a sigh.

'Gosh! Thank you. I promise I won't be too long. All I need are roses, and a weatherproof coat or jacket. How long could that possibly take?'

He returns my grin as he holds out his hand to me. I place mine in his, a tingle running through me as our flesh touches, and then he guides me across the gangway and on to the Boardwalk, where I quickly turn to face him.

He slowly releases my hand as if he doesn't want to let it go and as our fingers brush apart, there's a slight crease between his brows and an odd look in his eyes when they meet mine.

'Dad!' Eve calls out, breaking the spell. 'We nearly forgot this.' She's holding up the sickbag.

'I'll leave that in your Captain's capable hands,' I joke,' but it's definitely not part of my luggage.'

I laugh and wave my hand in the air as I walk away. I'm certain he is watching me and because of that, instead of rushing, I sashay in the sexiest way I can, but I dare not look back and check.

The sun is shining again here but there is a slight nip in the air. I suppose that's because of the rain and wind a few minutes earlier. Or possibly because, as this is a small island near the eastern end of the English Channel not far from the North Sea, it's more exposed to the sea breezes. I can only imagine what it's like here in the middle of winter. I'm not sure it's somewhere I'd want to be.

But then again, sitting in front of a roaring fire, wrapped in the arms of ...

I almost stumble; which serves me right. I must stop thinking about Ward Locke!

Even so, I now glance back over my shoulder, but he is no longer watching and I can't help feeling a little disappointed.

The first in the parade of shops on Boardwalk is, surprisingly enough, Locke Isle Tourist Office, or so it says on the purple-painted front door that matches the rest of the building. I wouldn't have thought an island this small would need a tourist office, but as it's currently closed, I have no way of finding out what it offers to tourists.

The second building is brightly painted yellow and green. I assume this must be the clothes shop Ward referred to as it has an evening gown and a suit in the small window. But the plaque that says: Frederick Dupont – Tailor, and Esther Dupont – Dressmaker would indicate that the owners of this shop make clothes to measure, and although that might be more in line with my preferred, shopping experience, it doesn't help me today. Nor does the fact that it is closed.

The florist, Buds and Blooms, painted orange, is third along and I want to check what time it closes, as I clearly need to go to the shops in Main Road for my weatherproof jacket or coat. The sign on the door says "We close at 5.00 p.m. so don't be late!" and it's as if that sign's been placed there just for me. Good thing I checked.

White Cliffs Café is the fourth along. It had looked welcoming from a distance with its blue façade, but as I get up close, it is even more so. Laughter burbles out through the open doorway and I have to take a sneaky peek inside. I see two women, possibly in their fifties, dancing together around the tables. They are both wearing white, starched aprons over black skirts and different coloured blouses, so they must work here, and the four customers I can see, are cheering them on. It's not at all the sort of place I would ever have considered going to for coffee, but when in Rome, as the saying goes. The odd thing is, as I walk away, I can't wait to return and get a proper look inside.

The final property in this parade is the convenience store and although I am tempted to go in and see if I can meet Ward's aunt, I really don't have time. I hurry back the way I came and then turn right and head towards Main Road.

The hill is steep and I'm glad I don't have my bags, but as I pass close to Nanny Tracy's, I wonder if I should briefly stop and say hello. I realise I don't have time, and I also don't have the flowers, so I continue on my way.

There's a T-junction ahead and when I reach it, Main Road splits to the left and right. To the right are some trees and a little further on, the road is lined with shops. To the left, the road leads to a long, tree lined drive that winds its way up a perfectly proportioned, circular mound in the centre of which Locke Keep proudly sits. The massive mound looks man-made, although I suppose it's possible it's a natural formation.

As I thought, Locke Keep is square with four imposing towers, one at each corner. A fifth, internal tower is smaller in circumference but slightly taller than the others and this is where the flag is flying from a white flag pole. I can't see the entrance to Locke Keep from here but I imagine it's impressive. I'd love to take a closer look at

Locke Keep but I don't have time right now.

The Keep is clearly centuries old and is definitely showing its age. Parts of the battlements on the tower nearest to me are gone and I assume it's the same with the others. I know how much it costs to maintain such ancient structures. McBriar Properties owns a few listed buildings and former stately homes, some of which we've refurbished, some of which we've rebuilt, and the sums involved are staggering. The amount of money Dad has spent on McBriar House alone over the years is eye-watering, even to people as wealthy as us. Judging by the battered ferry boat, the crumbling towers of Locke Keep, and the worn and faded clothes Ward is wearing, I can't help thinking that money may be a problem for the Lockes of Locke Isle.

Money is a genuine problem for many such families, or lack of it, I should say. Taxes, death duties, and time itself, all take their toll. Add the monumentally expensive annual maintenance costs, utility bills, staff salaries and such, and you don't have to be a genius to work out that a place like Locke Keep requires not only a small fortune to run, but determination, dedication, love, and a vast amount of, what Dad would call, 'true grit'. People dream of living in such places; the reality can be a nightmare if funds are limited. And even if they're not, owning this will be a constant struggle.

Ward's finances are not my problem. My mind should be fixed on finding myself a weatherproof coat.

I reluctantly turn away from Locke Keep and march purposefully towards the shops. Like the houses on this island, the façades of the shops are all brightly coloured. It makes shopping an even more delightful experience.

There are all types of shops here, several of which are artisan, and I am pleasantly surprised by the choice. From a craft shop to an art gallery, a toy shop to an electrical goods store – albeit it small. There's a bridal boutique, and a funeral director. That sends a shiver down my spine. Fortunately they are not next door to one another. There's a charity shop, and then I finally see the clothes store.

I want to shriek with delight, not because I'm thrilled by what I see, but simply because I've found it and it's open. It's called The Clothing Locker. I'm not sure if that's supposed to bear some connection to the fact that the island is called Locke Isle, or if it has nothing whatsoever to do with that.

'Hello!' I say as the bell above the door announces my arrival.

A young woman with scraped back, jet

black hair, long black eyelashes that are clearly false, and bright red lips that form a perfect 'O', pops her head out from between two, red velvet curtains, like a little bird in a cuckoo clock. 'I'll be with you in one minute,' she says, and her head darts back out of sight.

I wander around and look at each of the rails until I find what I'm looking for.

I'm not exactly spoilt for choice, and Ward is right about the labels, but at least there are a couple of items that appear to be in my size. I drop my handbag on to the grey, wood floor and try on a navy-blue jacket. It fits perfectly. I drape it over the rail and try on a purple raincoat. That's also a perfect fit.

Do I need both?

Of course I do.

And maybe one to fold up and put in my handbag. I've never had one of those before but the mannequin beside me is wearing one and it looks quite fetching on her.

I smile as I find one on the rail, and I remove it from the hanger and slip my arms inside. I feel as if it's sticking to my skin, and yet, it is lightweight, and it has a psychedelic pattern that appeals to me for some reason. Dad would hate it and so would Mum. Mum wouldn't have stepped inside this store. That helps me make up my mind, and as the sales assistant reappears, I hand her my three purchases.

'I'd like these, please. And may I wear this one now?'

'The psychedelic mac?' she queries, and looks startled by my burst of derisive laughter.

'Sorry. It's just that my ex was called Mack, so that made me laugh.'

'Was he a colourful character?'

I like her style. 'He was. Although not as colourful as this.'

'Are you sure you want all three? I know the weather has been naff, but are you expecting a lot of rain? They say better weather is on the way. Not that I'm trying to put you off buying them,' she adds hastily.

'Yes. I want all three ... please.'

She tells me the price and when I ask if she's sure that's right, she gives me a sympathetic smile.

'I know it's a lot. I wouldn't be able to afford all three either. We can put one back. Or two if you like. I can cancel the transaction and start again.'

'What? Oh no.' I laugh. 'I'm not bothered by the cost. I questioned it because it seems so little.' She raises her brows as if she doesn't agree and I realise I've committed a faux pas. She said she wouldn't be able to afford them, and I've just laughed and told her how cheap they are. 'I usually have to pay far more,' I add. 'And that's just for one.' Too late, it dawns on me that I've made things worse.

She clears her throat. 'Are you staying on Locke Isle, or just here on a day trip?'

'I've just arrived and I'm staying for a while.'

'At Castle Keep Hotel?'

'Sorry?'

'Is that where you're staying? At Castle Keep Hotel?'

'Erm. I didn't know Locke Keep was called that. Or that it's a hotel.'

'You're staying at Locke Keep!' She's almost shrieking now.

'No. I'm staying at a cottage on the cliffs, with friends. I think we're at cross purposes. Are Locke Keep and Castle Keep Hotel two separate places?'

'Erm, yeah.' She rolls her eyes but as I hand her my credit card, her eyes bulge. 'Wow! I've read about these cards, but I've never seen one.' She looks as if she wants to stroke it. And then she looks terrified. 'I'm so sorry! That was rude of me. Please don't make a complaint. I need this job.'

'I don't intend to. Don't worry.'

I've observed a slight raise of an eyebrow once or twice on the presentation of my card, but I have never seen anyone react quite like this. Then again, the staff at the establishments I usually frequent see exclusive cards like mine on a regular basis. Clearly this girl does not. It hits me that if this had happened a few months earlier, not only would I have probably made a complaint about her eye-roll, the "Er, yeah" comment, and her reaction to my card, I would have got her fired. But if this had been a couple of months ago, I wouldn't have been here.

'Thank you,' she says, breathing a genuine sigh of relief.

'You were telling me about Castle Keep Hotel,' I say, as she carefully folds my purchases. 'I should have guessed they weren't the same place. That was stupid of me. It's been a long day. I've travelled down from Edinburgh and ... sorry. Where's the hotel?' I cough, surprised by how much I had been about to tell her, and how much I already had.

'It's on the other side of the island, in Frenchman's Cove and it's the only luxury hotel here. Actually, it's the only hotel here. The Beacon Inn does B&B, and it's also the only pub. Not that you would be interested in a B&B. Or a pub. Erm ... When I saw your card, I assumed that was where you were staying. Although I've never seen one of these in real life before. You must be mega-rich to ... sorry!'

'Let's stop apologising, shall we? I'll have to take a look at this hotel. Does it have a spa?'

She nods. 'A really posh one.'

'Good. After the journey I've had, a massage would be divine.'

'Oh, you have to book in...' She laughs. 'Forget I said that. *You* won't have to book in advance. Not with a card like this.'

She hands it back to me, along with a carrier bag and my rainwear. I slip my purse back into my handbag, but not before I take out a twenty-pound note and a five-pound note, and then I put on the psychedelic shower mac.

'This is for the tip jar,' I say, dropping the fiver into the jar on the counter with a label stating: "Tips" and then I fold up the twenty-pound note and hand it to her. 'This is for you. Let's keep this conversation between us.'

She looks concerned. 'For me? Are you sure? Sorry. Are you famous? Should I know who you are? I'm not being rude. Honestly I'm not!'

'No! And I'd rather no one else knew who I was, either. Buy yourself a drink at that posh hotel.'

The colour drains from her face, apart from her bright red lips. 'Wow! Thank you. This is amazing. But ... if you don't mind, this will go towards my bills.'

'Oh. Of course. It's yours. Use it for whatever you want ... Natalie.' I've only just spotted her name badge.

She smiles in appreciation. 'Thank you so, so much. It was lovely to meet you. Have a good evening, and a wonderful time on Locke Isle.'

'Thanks.' I turn to leave and then I stop and turn to face her. 'Erm. I'm Gen ... with a G. Maybe I'll see you around, Natalie. Thank you for your help. And I want you to know, you're an exceptionally good sales assistant. You have a good evening too.'

She beams at me. 'Thank you. That means a lot to me. If there's anything you need while you're here, let me know and I'll see if I can help.'

'Thank you, Natalie.'

It seems Emma Barr was right. You do attract more bees with honey than with vinegar. And thinking of bees, I'd better hurry or the florist will be shut.

Seven

I dash into White Cliffs Café, having still not bought any replacement roses. I can't see Ward or Eve but that's not my main concern right now.

'Does anyone know where the florist is?' I blurt out, adding, 'Please,' as an afterthought.

One of the two women I'd seen dancing earlier is leaning on a counter. She stands upright and stares at me, shoving a pencil behind her ear as she says, 'Well, paint me green and call me a cucumber.'

I have no idea what that means, so I ignore her as the other woman appears from, what I assume must be, the kitchen, judging by the fact that she is carrying a tray of plates piled high with food. She is half in and half out, with her back holding the door open and she also stares at me.

'Next door,' she says, unhelpfully.

'I mean the actual person, not the shop,' I clarify.

'Ah, yes,' says the first woman, pointing to another woman sitting in deep conversation with an elderly man. 'Right there. Bernie! Someone wants you.'

'Who wants me, Sylvie?' Bernie asks.

'The beauty in the psychedelic mac.' Sylvie points at me.

Utterly bemused I say, 'I'd like some roses, please.'

'We don't sell roses,' the woman with the tray informs me. 'You want the florist, next door.'

'She knows that, Cece,' Sylvie tells her.

'I'm the florist,' says Bernie. 'But I'm on a date. Can you wait?'

I would laugh if this wasn't so ridiculous.

'I can. Except the sign on your door says you close at 5.00 p.m. and it's almost that now.'

'It's 4.50 p.m. by my watch,' says the elderly man sitting with Bernie.

'Oh my,' says Bernie. 'Doesn't time fly when you're having fun?'

Sylvie is studying me. 'Are you Gen ... with a G?'

'What? Yes, I am.'

'Ooohhh,' She draws out the word as they all look me up and down.

'Well he did say she is very pretty,' Cece

79

says.

I'm getting a little annoyed now. 'Sorry. But what, exactly, is going on here? And is there any chance that I might be able to buy some roses anytime soon?'

'The shop will be closing in ... nine minutes,' Bernie says, glancing at her own watch. 'If you want roses, you shouldn't be standing here taking that high and mighty tone. You should be next door, ringing the bell.'

'What bell?' I expel an exasperated sigh. 'Look. I apologise for my tone, but I would really like some flowers.'

What is wrong with these people? This is no way to run a business.

'The bell on the counter,' Bernie says. 'It clearly states: "Ring this bell for service if I'm not here." Did you ring the bell? Because I didn't hear it.'

'I didn't see a bell.'

'So you didn't ring it?'

'No!'

'Well you need to ring it. How else will I know you want to buy flowers?'

I want to shout, because I've just bloody well told you, you moron! Instead, I take several deep breaths and try to stay calm, and then I realise that Sylvie said my name just now, exactly the way Ward had.

'Did Ward Locke give you a message for

me?' I look Sylvie in the eye.

'Yes,' she nods.

'And...?'

'Oh. He said the second mate needed to pee. Please wait for them here.'

I sigh loudly. 'Thank you. And my luggage?'

'Your luggage?'

'He was bringing my luggage here, from the ferry.'

'Oh that. It's under the table over there.'

Sylvie points to a table in the window and I can now see my suitcase, holdall, and shopping bags.

'He left them here unattended!' I don't mean to shriek, but honestly. Who does that?

Sylvie quirks a brow and places a hand on her hip. 'Are you suggesting we can't be trusted?'

'I have no idea if you can or can't because I have no idea who any of you are!'

'Ward knows who we are. And he knows we can be trusted. If you trust him, you should trust us too.'

'There are four of us,' says the elderly gent.

Sylvie rolls her eyes. 'I meant, as well as, not, the number of people here, Alfred.'

'Oh right. Does the pretty little thing think we'd steal her belongings? Well, that's not cricket.'

They're clearly all mad. 'Look,' I say, feeling that my head may explode at any second. 'I'm sorry. It's been a long day. I apologise if I've caused offence.'

'Humph!' Sylvie says.

'May I please just buy some roses?' I plead with Bernie.

She looks at her watch again. 'I'll be closing in five minutes,' she says.

'I'll be quick, I promise.' She still doesn't move. 'Please!'

She crosses her arms in front of her chest. 'I still haven't heard the bell.'

'Arghhh!' I will murder her with the sodding bell!

I run to the florist shop, shove open the door, and thump my palm on the bell on the counter with all my might.

To my astonishment a charmingly pleasant voice says, 'Bernie will be with you shortly. Please look around while you wait.'

And now I do burst out laughing, although perhaps a little maniacally. And I'm still laughing when Bernie saunters in.

'What can I help you with today?' she says, in the sweetest tone possible as if we have never met.

'Roses?' I remind her. 'I want roses. Please.'

'I'm so sorry, but we're out of roses. I sold the last of them to a lovely local man about twenty minutes ago.'

How I don't throttle her is beyond me, but fortunately for Bernie, I hear Ward's voice and turn to see he's standing in the doorway.

'Gen?' he says. 'Is everything all right? You look a little ... flustered.' And then he looks me up and down and a crease forms between his brows. 'Did you ... did you buy that mac?'

'Yes. Why?'

'No reason. It's just not what I was expecting.'

'Come to collect your flowers, Ward?' Bernie coos.

She hands him two huge bouquets of roses. One of twenty red roses just like the ones I'd bought for Nanny Tracy, and one of twelve yellow roses, which I have to say are far more beautiful than the red ones, as there are various shades of yellow and tinges of orange in each rose.

'You bought the last of the roses!' I glare at him.

'For you,' he says. 'Well, not for you, exactly. At least, not the red ones. They're to replace the ones that went overboard. In case Bernie ran out. It is Friday, and lots of people buy flowers on Fridays.'

'That's true,' says Bernie. 'They do. Alfred bought flowers for me for our date.

83

And I did run out of roses.'

I give her a tight smile, and a much friendlier one to Ward. I want to hug him, but I stop myself.

'Oh, Ward. That is so kind of you. Thank you.'

He coughs, and to my surprise, he hands the yellow bouquet to me. 'These are for you.'

'For me?' I shift the carrier bag containing my new rainwear into the crook of my arm so that I can take them from him. My fingers brush against his for a second, sending those increasingly familiar tingles shooting through me. 'They're beautiful. Thank you. But why?'

'Why? Oh. As a ...' He runs his free hand through his hair. 'Erm ... as a welcome to Locke Isle.'

I raise my brows. 'Gosh. That's lovely. Do you welcome everyone to Locke Isle with flowers? Is it a tradition?'

'First I've heard of it,' Bernie says. 'Before today, the last time you bought flowers was–'

'Weren't you on a date with Alfred?' Ward cuts her short.

'Yes. And having the time of my life.'

'Don't you want to get back to it?'

'If you two will let me shut up my shop, I will.'

Ward smiles at her. 'Sorry, Bernie. We'll

get out of here.' He reaches out his free hand and I place my own free hand in his. 'Did you get what you wanted? Shopping-wise, I mean.'

'I did, thanks. You don't like this mac, I assume?'

'I do! It's very ... colourful.'

I smile contentedly. 'It is. That's why I bought it. Where're Eve and Horatio?' I suddenly realise they're not with him.

'They went on ahead to next door. I saw you run in here so I thought I'd better tell you I'd already bought the flowers.'

'I'm going to pay you for them. The red ones, at least.'

He opens the shop door for me, and Bernie comes to lock it behind us, pulling down a blind behind the glass door.

'No. They're a gift.'

'Precisely! The red ones are a gift from me to Nanny Tracy. If you pay for them then they'll be a gift from you, not from me.'

'Hmm. Okay, I get that. Fine. You can pay for the coffees.'

'I've already said I'll pay for those. So I need to pay for something else. Why won't you just let me pay you for the flowers?'

'Okay! I will.'

'Ward?' I stop before we reach the door to White Cliffs Café.

'Yes?' He looks nervous.

'This sounds pathetic. Especially coming from me. But ... the people in here weren't ... that welcoming. And one said to paint her green and call her a cucumber. What on earth does that mean?'

He snorts a laugh. 'That's Sylvia. Or Sylvie, as we all call her. And that's her favourite saying. It means something is cool, or that she is cool with whatever is happening. She wouldn't have meant it to upset you.'

'She made the comment when I walked in.'

'Then it probably meant she liked your psychedelic, showerproof mac.'

'Are you making fun of me?'

'No! I'm serious.'

'They ... they also got a bit upset when I asked why you'd left my things unattended.'

I realise the irony of that, as I'd just done the same thing myself.

'Ah, yes. That would be irksome. Both Sylvie and Cece, or Celia to use her given name, think trust is terribly important, so you'll have some making up to do for that. And Alfred is their older brother, so he feels the same. He and Bernie are on their first date today, so Bernie may be acting a little weird. Her husband died three years ago, and she's known Alfred all her life, but she told me the other day that she felt like a teenager again when Alfred asked her out. His own wife passed away at least ten years ago, but he's always had a soft spot for Bernie. I suppose it's my fault. About the luggage, I mean. I shouldn't have left until you arrived. The problem was, Horatio needed to pee, and then Eve wanted to toss stones into the water, and although this island is safe, I don't like letting her run around on the beach alone, especially during holiday season. You can never be too careful with young kids. Erm. Sorry. I appear to be waffling.'

'I understand. I'll apologise to them again.'

He smiles. 'Not something you're used to doing?'

'You have no idea.'

He laughs, and squeezes my hand in a reassuring gesture, and then an expression of something akin to shock and horror spreads rapidly over his face. He looks down at our clasped hands and quickly lets go of mine. 'I'm so sorry! he exclaims. 'I didn't realise ... that is, I forgot ... Erm ... I didn't mean to hold your hand. At least not for so long.'

His words take me by surprise but not as much as the sheer terror in his eyes.

'It's okay, Ward. It's not the end of the world. And it doesn't mean we're married or anything.' I'm trying to sound light hearted, but I feel a little hurt. Holding hands with

Ward seemed the most natural thing in the world.

But now I can see why he might be worried. He is a married man after all.

Although ... he has just bought me roses. And he handed them to me in front of Bernie.

I'm confused as he pushes open the door of White Cliffs Café, and even more so as he reaches his hand out to me, yet again, and then hastily retracts it.

'You can do this,' he says. 'And they're all lovely people, once you get to know them. Ready?'

I take a deep breath. 'Ready as I'll ever be.'

I've never felt less ready for anything in my life. Today has certainly been an entirely new experience for me.

And it's not over yet.

Eight

'Paint me green and call me a cucumber,' Sylvie says, once again, but this time I smile. 'You're back. And with your roses, I see.'

'Yes,' I say. 'And I apologise again for earlier. Of course my things are safe with you. Ward wouldn't have left them here otherwise.'

'That's what we said.' Sylvie nods but now she's also smiling at me. Or perhaps smirking is more apt. 'And as you ran off and left them just now, you can hardly berate him, can you?' She shrugs. 'But you're a newcomer to the island, so we can forgive a few slip-ups. What are you having?'

'Just coffee for me, please.'

I know there is no point in asking for a special blend. I can see from what the other customers are drinking that this is the kind of café where tea comes in mugs, and coffee comes black or with milk, and that's it.

'Coffee for me too, please,' says Ward. 'Are you sure that's all you want?' he asks me.

'Yes, thanks. I had a big lunch.' He raises his brows, and we both laugh, the embarrassment of the hand-holding incident now replaced with memories of my earlier embarrassment. 'I'm still not hungry,' I assure him.

He glances over to the table where Eve is sitting, and so do I. Horatio is curled up beside my belongings.

'I see Eve has more ice cream.' He shakes his head but he's smiling. She had obviously had some earlier, before they took Horatio for his pee. 'In that case, I'll have a slice of your delicious banana bread, please. And a slice to take home.'

That hits me like a comet. He's taking home a slice of banana bread ... for his wife! The man was just holding my hand! And he's bought me flowers!

No wonder these people have contempt for me.

Does he do this a lot?

And yet. The cake might be for someone else.

Would he really flaunt his latest conquest, in his local café?

I'm not his conquest.

Yet.

But he knows I'm attracted to him. And

he's clearly attracted to me, despite what he said about us holding hands.

Although, not to be big-headed, most men *are* attracted to me. There's no point in denying that. Mainly for my beauty and my perfect body, of course. But some men are also attracted by the fact that I embody class and style, and I know exactly what to wear for every occasion.

The shower mac I'm wearing now is a first. And probably a last.

Men are also attracted by my walk – like on Boardwalk this afternoon. I knew Ward would be watching me, because men always do. And some women, too. I sway my hips seductively but naturally (again thanks to Mum teaching me her catwalk tips) and heads always turn as I glide gracefully even on the highest heels.

Men are also attracted by my glossy, waist-length, brunette hair, and even when I wear it up in a loose bun, or a tight chignon, or a plait, it always looks sensational, because Raymondo, my hairstylist, is a true artiste. Although today it's somewhat windswept, and Raymondo, would have an apoplexy if he saw me.

My voice is another quality men find incredibly attractive. I had a voice coach from the age of eight, so not only do I know how to speak the King's English as precisely as a Queen, if I so choose, I know the correct and most appropriate tone to use for every occasion. Even my laugh has been trained. I can be sexy and seductive, warm and caring, friendly or terrifying, or mysterious and full of promise.

In fact, now that I think about it, I'm a bit like a trained monkey, only taller, wealthier, and with a more extensive vocabulary.

That's a rather depressing thought, and one that has never occurred to me before today.

But it's not nearly as depressing as the thought that Ward Locke has a wife.

'Are you okay?' he asks.

'I'm fine.' I march to the table and sit.

'This ice cream is yummy,' Eve says. 'Want some?'

She offers me a spoonful of ice cream but I shake my head, and say, 'No, thank you.' Firstly because, one should not eat food from another person's cutlery. Secondly because, I've had enough temptation for one day. Mainly in the shape of a tall, broad-shouldered hunk of a man who has somehow made me fall for him within the space of one afternoon. Less than an afternoon. More like a couple of hours. No. Even less.

Oh cripes! To use an expression that Nanny Tracy used to say. I could be in trouble here.

I'm not saying I'm in love with him. Of course I'm not. But I'm certainly in lust. And I like him very much.

Too much.

Far too much.

We've even been holding hands!

Who does that with a man they've only just met?

And yet, I did sleep with Mack on the night we met. Within a couple of hours of meeting him, in fact.

And look how that turned out.

There's clear precedent for me and this type of behaviour.

But is that why Ward pulled away? Is he feeling for me, what I'm feeling for him?

What am I feeling for him?

Do I simply want to go to bed with him? Do I want a summer fling? Am I using him to mend my broken heart and to get over Mack?

So much for me changing my ways.

Ward joins us and he's studying me intently. A part of me wants to shout at him to go home to his bloody wife!

Unfortunately, a larger part of me wants to keep him here with me for as long as possible. How ridiculous is that?

'I need the toilet,' Eve says, suddenly jumping up and squeezing past me.

'Hey!' Sylvie shrieks, as Eve almost

knocks the tray from her hands. 'She's a bundle of energy, isn't she?' Sylvie places the tray on our table and slides it across so that my coffee is in front of me and Ward's coffee and banana bread is in front of him.

'I'm paying for these,' I say, reaching for my purse.

Sylvie gives me an odd look and points to a notice on the wall.

"Don't pay, don't stay."

'I don't understand,' I say.

'It's already paid for,' she says. 'We take payment when you order, not after.'

'Oh! I'm sorry.'

'It's fine,' says Ward, grinning. 'You can get it next time.'

'Enjoy,' says Sylvie, and wanders off to serve other customers.

'Is there going to be a next time?' I ask.

Ward seems both concerned and confused. 'I hope so. I mean ... I'm sure there will be. I haven't asked how long you plan to stay, but I'd like to see you again. Erm ... that is, I'll see you around on the island. It's not a massive place, after all. We ... we're bound to bump into one another again. If you'd like that too, of course. Have coffee. Not bump into...' He laughs awkwardly and runs a hand through his hair. 'I seem to be all tongue-tied today. I think what I'm trying to say is that I would like to have coffee with you again while you're here.'

'I'd like that too,' I say. 'Erm. I should've asked. Your wife won't mind you being late because of me, will she? Or aren't you intending to tell her?'

I don't know why I said it like that. Why couldn't I have casually asked about his marital status? Why hadn't I simply said, 'I assume you're no longer married.'

He looks as if I've slapped his face. He's taken aback and his brows knit together as his eyes search mine. The colour drains from his cheeks and his mouth falls open but nothing comes out. He appears genuinely shocked and it's a moment before he responds. His voice is low and scratchy as if he's having trouble with the words.

'My wife?' He leans closer. 'I ... my wife is dead! I thought you knew that. Are you ... are you saying you didn't? Are you telling me that you believed I was married and yet you ... you flirted with me?'

'Flirted with you? I didn't flirt with you!'

'Shush!' he commands. 'I don't want everyone to hear. Please keep your voice low.'

'Yes, oh Lord and Master!' I lean forward and softly hiss, 'If anyone flirted here, it was you who flirted with me.'

He moves closer still. 'Seriously? So you didn't check me out the second you boarded my ferry? And you didn't give me those come

95

to bed eyes when you slid your sunglasses down your beautiful nose? And you didn't try to turn me on by falling against me in the wheelhouse and then making sure our bodies brushed against one another's as we docked? You weren't walking down the Boardwalk in the most seductive way you could? Oh, and you weren't just holding my hand less than five minutes ago? None of that was you? None of that was flirting?'

He's certainly not tongue-tied now. Damn him.

'Fine. I'll admit I thought you were ... attractive. And I might've done a couple of the things you said. But I thought you might've been married, so I tried to pull back. But then you kept being nice, and kind, and ... lovely. And I liked you. I hoped you were divorced, or separated or something, but you never said a word about it.'

'I thought you knew.'

'Based on what? Why would I know?'

'I assumed Tracy would've told you. Why didn't you simply ask?'

I sigh. 'I don't know. And I assumed you wanted to sleep with me, and you'd see how far you could get.'

'See how far I could get?' His voice increases a fraction and then it's back to a whisper. 'So ... are you saying you'd sleep with a man you thought was still living with his wife, even though they had a child?'

'No! I ... I don't think so. I've never done that before.'

'How far would you have gone?'

'I don't know, okay? I liked you. And I'm not thinking rationally right now. But that's why I asked about your wife. How was I to know she's dead? Oh! I'm so sorry about that, by the way. When did she...? Sorry!' I raise my hands in front of my chest. 'Forget I asked. That sounded awful even to me.'

'Really? That sounded like the Geneva McBriar I've heard about. The woman who knows what she wants and knows how to get it. The woman who only thinks of herself and her own happiness. Oh, and her father's, property empire, of course. I don't know why I'm so surprised. Or so disappointed. This is all just a game to you, isn't it? You're simply a bored, little rich girl, who treats everyone around her as her own personal toy. You even pretended to like Eve. And Horatio.'

'I didn't pretend! And I'm not "a bored little rich girl". Although I am getting bored with this!' My voice is growing louder and I have to tone it down. Heads are turning to look at us. I lower my voice to match Ward's own angry whisper. 'I do like Eve. And I do like Horatio. Look. I told you I was trying to change. I told you that was why I'm here. I didn't come here to have a casual fling with some hot guy who runs the local, bloody ferry.'

'Roughing it, were you?'

'Roughing it? You have no idea. Sorry! I didn't mean that the way it came out.'

'I think you did.'

'As you've known me for about, oh, I don't know, two hours, I can safely say you don't know anything about me, or what I think. Not the real me.'

'Is there a real you? Yes, I think there is. And that's a stunningly beautiful woman called Geneva. I liked Gen. With a G. She seemed friendly and kind, and she had a sense of humour and self-deprecation. But she was still beautiful and sexy, only not in a fake way, like Geneva.'

'Fake way! There's nothing fake about me. What you see is what you get. And every inch of me is real.' His eyes flicker over my body for a second. 'As you might've found out if you weren't so damn ... fickle.'

'Fickle?' His angry gaze meets mine. 'I'm not fickle. I'm simply ... confused. I felt something today that I ... that I haven't felt for a long, long time. And it felt good. But I'll admit I was torn. I don't have time for relationships. I've got Eve to think about and she means everything to me. And then there's this island and everyone on it. I've got struggling businesses to run, a crumbling home to maintain. Falling for someone isn't part of my plan, and it isn't an option for me right now. I'm not sure when it will be. I need to put other people's interests before mine. But ... you ... I mean Gen, seemed interested in me. And in my daughter and our dog. And I ... I let my guard down, and maybe for a moment ... a brief and beautiful moment, I actually thought there might be something ... between us. It's such a shame that Gen's not real. But then again, it's not. As I said. I don't have time for romance.'

'Romance? Or sex? I saw the way you looked at me. The way you're still looking at me, despite all your sanctimonious claptrap. You just wanted to get me into bed.'

'Sanctimonious claptrap? You're saying you don't believe me?'

I lean even closer and our faces are almost touching across the table as I summon up the sexiest tone I can.

'I'm saying that if I said, right now, right this minute, that I'd have sex with you, you'd be out of that seat and grabbing my hand again, and rushing me up to one of your crumbling turrets to have your way with me. And don't deny it, because we both know that, at least, is the truth.'

His eyes narrow for a second. 'I'm a man, not a monk. Of course I'd have sex with you. Who wouldn't? I mean, look at you. But that's the problem. Or not. As we now know, Gen doesn't exist. I'd have sex with Geneva and I'm sure I'd enjoy every moment of it. I think I can safely say we both would. I would probably even want to do it again. But it would just be sex. What I felt today, with the woman I thought was Gen, wasn't just about sex. It was ... well, it doesn't matter what it was. I'm not entirely sure I know. But what I do know is that if Gen were real, whatever happened between us would've been about more than just having sex. And that's why I was scared. I've never believed in love at first sight but for a moment today I...' He shakes his head and inhales a quick breath. 'No. I think I was simply blown away by your beauty, and then intoxicated by your charm. I was moved by your vulnerability, and the concern you showed over replacing some flowers. But none of that was real, was it? None of that was true.'

'Da-ad!' Eve's voice startles us both and I turn to see her standing just a few feet away from our table.

'How long have you been there?' Ward asks, his astonishment apparent.

'Ages,' she says, sliding one foot from side to side on the black and white check, tiled floor.

'Did you ... did you hear what we were saying?'

She shakes her head. 'You were whispering. Nanny Tracy says it's rude to listen when people are whispering 'cos it means they have a secret or something they don't want anyone else to hear. But I'm bored now and so is Horatio. Look.'

She points to the black Labrador who is curled beneath the table, and currently looking up at us. Both Ward and I had completely forgotten he was there. Our eyes meet once again but only for a moment and then Ward looks away and smiles at Eve.

'I'm so sorry, honey. Would you like a milkshake?'

Her curls bounce from side to side as she vigorously shakes her head and then she contradicts her action by saying, 'Yes, please. But I'm hungry, Dad. Can we stay here for supper, please? Cece said they've got my favourite pizza. And they've got food for Horatio, too. Please Daddy.'

For a split second she reminds me of the young me. It's the way she's clasping her fingers in front of her tummy and looking all doe-eyed at her dad. But then she chuckles and swings to and fro. Something I would never have done when asking Dad for anything.

Ward gives her a massive and farcical frown and then he leans over and tickles her and she roars with laughter. He pulls her to him, firmly but gently, and lifts her on to his lap, encircling her with his arms as he kisses her loudly on her head. That makes her squeal with delight and everyone in the café watches them and smiles, oddly enough, including me.

'Of course we can,' he says, and the love in his eyes is unmistakeable. He kisses her once more and then gently stands her on her feet. 'Go and tell Cece we're staying.'

Eve rushes off and Horatio bounds after her. Ward watches her go, and then he looks at me and there's an unfathomable expression on his face as he expels a lengthy sigh.

'Cece won't be pleased if Horatio goes in to the kitchen,' he says, and then adds, 'You're welcome to join us.'

I can't believe it. After all the things we've just said to one another, he's inviting me to stay for pizza and milkshake!

'No thanks,' I say. 'I think it's time I left. It's such a shame that the man I just witnessed doing all that is the same man that said such awful things about me. It seems the Lord of Locke Isle also has two faces, and he is not a true gentleman. Nor sadly, is he rich enough to employ someone to run his bloody ferry. Because if he had been, perhaps we wouldn't have met! And we wouldn't have had this argument.' I grab my purse and toss ten, twenty-pound notes across the table. 'That should cover the flowers, the coffees, the cake, and ice cream. Keep the rest as a tip. Or to pay for supper. And here's another tip. Next time you want to sleep with a woman you've just met, be smart enough to tell her at the start, you're no longer married.'

I leap to my feet, grab my suitcase, throw my holdall on my shoulder, and shove the shopping bags on my arm as he watches me in silence. It's only when I reach for the roses, that he speaks again.

'Geneva? Gen!' His voice sounds strangled, desperate, contrite.

He stretches his hand out for mine but I snatch it away and glare at him.

'Don't! Just don't. We've said all that needs to be said. I hope we don't meet again. And as for me getting back to the mainland, I'll find alternative transport. As you're well aware, I *can* afford it.'

He shoves the money towards me. 'I don't want this.'

'Take it. You can buy someone else some yellow roses. I'm taking these because I've paid for them. Have a good life, Ward, and good luck with your ... plan. Say goodbye to Eve and Horatio for me.'

'You can do that yourself,' he says, and then sighs again as he starts to get to his feet. 'This is ridiculous. Let me help you with your luggage.'

'No!' I glower. 'Stay and enjoy your supper. I mean it, Ward. And this is Geneva McBriar speaking. The *real* Geneva McBriar. Believe me, she is not a woman you want to mess with.' I turn and walk away.

'You're leaving?' Sylvie calls out as I drag my suitcase to the door.

I can feel all eyes are on me, but I don't care. I am Geneva McBriar and I've run gauntlets far tougher than this one. Eve is nowhere to be seen but I assume she's in the kitchen with Cece and Horatio, sorting out their supper.

'Yes,' I say. 'I am. It's been ... enlightening.'

'Well, paint me green and call me a cucumber,' Sylvie says, and I almost laugh.

'Ward?' Alfred booms across the café. 'Why aren't you helping the young lady with her bags?'

'Because the *lady* doesn't want me to,' Ward snaps, with a particularly cold emphasis on the word, lady. 'She doesn't need any help. She can do anything she wants.'

'Well,' says Alfred. 'That's not cricket.'

'You know where I am if you ever need flowers,' Bernie calls out. The other five or six people in the café either tut or groan, and I can imagine what they'll all say about me as

I slam the door behind me.

I am fuming as I march along Boardwalk, but I'm crying by the time I stagger up the hill.

And it's not just because my bags are heavy and I've been unused to carrying my own luggage, until today.

Nine

'Oh my goodness!' Nanny Tracy says, beaming as she opens the front door of White Cliffs Cottage. 'Is it really you, Geneva? Oh, sweetheart! Have you been crying? What's happened? Where's Ward? Come in, my love. Roger! Geneva's here and she's upset. Bring the brandy, darling.'

'I'm so, so sorry, Nanny!' I drop my luggage in the hall, and sob on her shoulder as she pulls me into a tight hug. She is several inches shorter, so I'm bending down, and it's not the most comfortable position.

'Don't apologise to me, sweetheart. Come and sit on the sofa and tell us all about it. Roger will pour you a brandy and he'll put the kettle on, and then he'll take your bags to your room. Roger, this is Geneva.'

I lift my head and see an elderly man standing in the hall, dressed casually but smartly in grey flannel trousers, a white cotton shirt and a grey cardigan. I believe Nanny Tracy is in her mid-sixties, but I can't exactly recall. Roger must be late seventies, or even early eighties, yet he's still a handsome man. He looks kind and the expression on his face shows signs of genuine empathy.

'Hello, Geneva. I'm glad to finally meet you but I wish you weren't upset. Is there anything I can do? I'm a good listener, just like Tracy, but if you'd rather spend some time alone with just my darling wife, you go ahead, and don't mind me. Here's a glass of brandy. I'll take the bottle into the sitting room in case more is needed.'

'Hello, Roger,' I say, sniffing slightly. 'It's lovely to meet you. I'm sorry to arrive like this. And I'm sorry I didn't come here right away. But I dropped the roses in the sea and I wanted to get fresh ones, because I know Nanny loves roses. Oh, these are for you, Nanny.' I reach down and retrieve the red roses, which I hand to her.

'Thank you, sweetheart. But you didn't need to get me these. Seeing you is the only gift I need.'

'Oh why am I such a fool, Nanny?'

'You're not a fool, sweetheart. And now that you're a grown woman, I think it's time you called me Tracy, don't you? Unless you want to call me Nanny, in which case that's fine.'

'Erm. I don't know,' I sob. 'Nanny is comforting, somehow. But then again, Tracy is friendly, and I do need a friend right now.'

'Well call me either. Or both. I don't mind at all. And you'll have both comfort and friendship from me and from Roger, so don't you worry about that. Now drink your brandy and come and sit with me. Roger, darling, if you don't mind, I think it's best if you go to the Watershed for a while. Just until Geneva has settled.'

'Of course I don't mind. Call me if you want anything. I'll put those beautiful roses in a vase, and take your things upstairs.'

He takes the bouquet from his wife and I step back a little as he kisses her on the cheek. The smiles they exchange are so full of love, I start to sob again, but I try to control myself.

I don't know what's the matter with me. I can't remember the last time I cried. I'm not that sort of person. I don't burst into tears just because I've argued with a man. At least I didn't until today. I haven't even really cried over Mack. I was angry, yes, and vengeful too. But tearful? No. And I loved Mack. I don't love Ward, so why am I crying?

Perhaps that is the problem. Maybe these tears are for Mack, and for the loss of the relationship and friendship I thought we shared. I usually vent my feelings with anger and revenge, just like Dad. But it's normally controlled anger and cold, calculated revenge. I've never been an emotional wreck before. Never. And yet, that is what I appear to be right now.

Emma Barr's comments stirred up feelings and emotions in me that had been buried for many years. Her words also made me halt my vengeful actions against Mack, and take a good, hard look at myself instead. Add all that to the heartbreak I felt over losing Mack – heartbreak I tried hard to keep hidden, and perhaps this has been building for a couple of months.

Maybe this has less to do with Ward Locke and the sudden and unexpected feelings he aroused in me today, and more to do with all the years of loneliness, the lack of love from Mum and Dad, mixed with a cocktail of heartbreak over Mack, and self-loathing brought to the surface by Emma's lecture.

Wow! Have I become one of those people who blames her parents, and everyone else for her predicament? My upbringing made me the adult I became, but as an adult, I've had many years to take control of my own life and change the things I didn't like, so I can't lay all the blame at everyone else's feet.

And isn't that why I'm here? To change? To face who I am and what I've become? To rid myself of the things I don't like about myself, and work hard to improve the things I do? Maybe tears are part of all that. Perhaps this is what I need to do.

Gosh. Self-awareness is tough. But then again, so am I. Geneva McBriar may have many qualities that aren't very pleasant, but one good quality I do have is resilience. And another is strength.

'You don't have to go on my account,' I say. 'What ... what's the Watershed?'

I wonder if it's an outside toilet or something equally awful.

'It's a bar,' Nanny Tracy says, with a loving smile. 'It's one of those contrivances that folds away and looks like a small, wooden shed when it's closed, but opens into a nifty bar, complete with shelves, enough space for small barrels and several bottles, a fold down table or bar top, and two stools. It's in the back garden, hidden amongst the gladioli and the wisteria. We often sit out there. Especially if it's sunny, or a balmy summer night. Or during the day, Roger sits out there and listens to the cricket, or has some friends round while I'm at Bingo in the Church Hall.'

'It sounds lovely.' Oddly enough, it does.

'It's painted red, white and blue, in

vertical stripes,' Roger informs me. 'Did it myself, last summer. And my darling wife made bunting to match. We have a string of fairy lights in the same colours, and some battery-operated candles, just to add a touch of romance once it's dark.' He sounds proud of it, and of Nanny Tracy.

I must stop calling her that, she's right. I am an adult. Nanny was what the young me called her. Nanny Tracy is the comfort that grown child needed, so as I want to become a better woman, I think I should be an adult about this and call her Tracy.

'I'd like to see it,' I say. 'If you don't mind, that is.'

'Mind? Why would we mind?' He puffs out his cheeks as if the very thought of either of them minding, is preposterous. 'Of course you can see it. Why don't you and Tracy have a chat and then both come and join me in the garden when you're ready? I think the rain is gone for the night and there'll be clear skies at least until morning. We should get to see plenty of stars. Nothing like myriad celestial bodies to make us realise what's really important. Oh, I don't mean whatever has upset you, isn't important, my dear. I just mean that staring at the heavens can help us see more clearly sometimes. It helps us put things into perspective.' He coughs. 'I'll shut up and leave you to it.' He winks and smiles as he gently pats my arm, in a grandfatherly gesture that's surprisingly comforting. Just like one of my former nanny's hugs.

'He's wonderful,' I say when I'm sure he's out of earshot.

Tracy sighs. 'He certainly is. I thank my lucky stars for the day we met.'

She takes my hand and leads me into the cosy sitting room. It is compact but large enough to house a plump and comfy, but well worn, floral-patterned sofa, on which we sit side by side. There are small side tables at each end, both with lamps, the shades of which match the sofa. A plain blue rug sits in front of a brick fireplace with a stone mantelpiece where a clock ticks in the centre. Either side of the fireplace are bookcases and shelves teeming with hardback books, framed photos, and ornaments.

One of the photos is of me blowing out four candles on a massive birthday cake, another is of me, aged around five or six, building a sandcastle on a beach, with Nanny's help. And a third is of both of us putting presents beneath the family, Christmas Tree. That was the last Christmas we spent together, before Dad sent us both away. Me, to boarding school. Tracy to ... I don't know where she went when she left. And that makes me sad. I nearly burst into tears yet again, but I fight them back.

She hasn't changed much over the years, apart from growing older. She still has blonde, wavy, shoulder-length hair, although there is a smattering of grey running through it now. She's still slim and petite, and she has retained her beauty, and her freckles. Her smile is even more loving than I remember.

'How did you meet?' I sip the brandy and wipe my eyes, having finally regained control of my emotions. I want to hear this story.

'Funnily enough, we met on the Locke Isle Ferry. Roger was the ferryman back then. A job he held until this year, when he decided it was time he retired. He was so handsome. And so strong.'

She sighs at the memory, and I try to hide my surprise over his job. Ward hadn't mentioned that. He hadn't mentioned many things, it seemed.

'So Roger was employed by Ward, and before that, by Ward's family, for more than twenty years, until last year?' If Tracy and Roger met on the ferry, it must've been more than twenty, because they married twenty years ago.

Tracy nods. 'Ward's father employed him, and Ward kept Roger on after his father died. Roger should've retired years ago, but he would've gone on forever if he could have. Ward allowed him to continue working, all the while Roger wanted to, but Ward had been helping more and more over the last few years, and Roger had one or two little accidents on board. Nothing serious. He missed his footing on the ladder and twisted his ankle. And he caught his hand in a rope and broke his wrist. Ward didn't want him to continue taking chances. He said he'd never forgive himself if something serious happened to my darling man, so both Ward and I suggested it might be time Roger took things easy, and he finally agreed. Roger often goes out with Ward, though, if the weather is good. Ward does all the work now, of course, and Roger just sits and enjoys the journey and Ward's company.'

I appear to have misjudged Ward Locke, or at least certain aspects of his character. The thought brings tears to my eyes yet again and I blink them back. I am not crying over this. I am not!

'Tell me more about the day you met. If you're happy to share details.'

'I'm more than happy to. It was a lovely sunny, summer's day, but it had rained in the morning. Oh! It was a bit like this one, weatherwise. It was the first trip of the day and I was the only passenger. I was coming over for the day to have a look around. I was staying with a friend in Folkestone but she was working that day. It was a Monday, and I was supposed to be returning on the last trip that afternoon. Roger said he thought the weather might turn, and he was right. A storm came out of nowhere and Roger told me to join him in the wheelhouse. We were more than halfway across, so it was safer to continue here than to turn back. For a moment, I feared for my life because the ferry was lurching and rolling and the waves were crashing over the main deck. But Roger told me not to worry and he'd get me to Locke Isle safe and sound. I said I'd pay for the best steak meal ever, if he did. He'd told me a plate of steak and chips was his favourite meal.' She smiled. 'He got me here safe and sound, and took me to White Cliffs Café for coffee. The storm raged all morning and it was set in for the day, and as he couldn't take the ferry out, we sat and talked for several hours. Later, we went for the best steak and chips on the island, at Fifi's Cuisine. That was the name of the restaurant on Main Street. And it's still there. After lunch, Roger was going to help me find a place to stay for the night as I clearly wasn't getting back to the mainland.' She gives a small cough and a rosy glow spreads across her cheeks. 'Now don't think badly of me, Geneva, but Roger was not only handsome, he was kind and thoughtful, and ... there's no point in denying it, I fancied the man like crazy.'

'I can understand why. He's a very

handsome man.'

She beams at me. 'He is, isn't he? And you should've seen him back then. Wait.'

She stands up and takes a large framed photo from the wall behind us. It's of their wedding day and they both look so happy and so in love that my heart does a little flip.

'I wish I had been there,' I say. 'You look beautiful, and Roger was really hot, you're right. You look completely in love and extremely happy.'

'We were. We still are. I wish you'd been there too. But you were always in my heart, Geneva, so in a way, you were at our wedding.'

She kisses the tips of her fingers, taps them against Roger's face in the photo, and then smiles lovingly, as she places the framed photo back on its hook on the wall and spends several seconds ensuring it's perfectly balanced.

'I am so sorry I didn't get in touch,' I say. 'I know I've said that before, but I really do mean it. I wish I had. I don't know why I didn't.'

'You're here now, sweetheart. That's all that matters.'

I smile at her and then nudge her elbow. 'So what happened next? You were saying Roger was going to help you find somewhere to stay, and that I shouldn't think badly of you. I assume that means you spent the night with him.'

She lets out a swoony sigh. 'I did. And it was utterly wonderful. He suggested the hotel, on the other side of the island, and then he said, "Or there's a guest room in my cottage." Of course we both hoped I would spend the night in his room, not the guest room, but neither of us wanted to say that. I immediately said I'd love to stay in his guest room, and we ran all the way here. It was raining buckets, so we used that as an excuse for our haste to get inside. The moment he closed the front door behind us, we looked at one another and we fell into each other's arms. The man swept me off my feet. Literally. He carried me upstairs and we ... we spent the entire afternoon making love, while the rain lashed the roof and windows and the gale force winds made the house and everything in it, shake ... including Roger's bed!' She winks at me and I burst out laughing.

'Nanny Tracy! What a naughty girl you are. That shaking bed had nothing to do with the weather, did it? Well, well.' I reach across and squeeze her hand. 'I'm delighted for you, Tracy. I truly am. And for Roger too.'

She blushes again. 'I surprised myself. I had never done anything like that before in my life. But it was as if I knew, almost from the moment I saw him, that he was the man for me. And I didn't make it back to my friend's house until a few days later. I blamed the weather – which was bad for several days so that was partly true, but she knew it was because I didn't want to leave Roger. I had called her that first evening, to let her know I was safe, and I told her I'd met someone. She was happy for me, and told me not to rush back if I didn't want to. I really didn't want to. I did return eventually, but only for one day, to collect my belongings. Roger asked me to move in with him and I did. I haven't regretted that decision for one second. That storm was a gift from the gods. And so is Roger. I love the man with my heart and soul. I truly hope that one day, sweetheart. One day very soon, you'll find yourself with a man like Roger. Only a younger version now, of course.' She grins. 'And I hope you'll be as happy and as fulfilled with him as I am with my darling man.'

Now it's me who sighs. I can't help thinking of the similarities between how she met Roger, and my afternoon with Ward Locke. Except our meeting didn't have a happy ending like theirs.

'I hope so too,' I say.

Now she's the one who squeezes my hand. 'Are you ready to tell me why you were crying?'

I nod. I had already told her, during our telephone conversation when I first got back in touch, snippets of what I'd been doing since we parted ways, but now I tell her everything that's happened this year. I briefly explain how I first met Mack, then fill her in on the fake engagement, my hopes and dreams, what really happened, and then how and why it ended. After that I tell her about Emma Barr, and everything she said to me and how it made me feel. I explained about my epiphany and what I wanted to achieve. And I finally get around to telling her what happened from the moment I stepped on the ferry today, until the moment I arrived at her door. I also say how strange I've been feeling and that I can't understand why I keep wanting to burst into tears.

'Goodness me,' she says when I eventually finish. 'The way you met Ward is so similar to what happened to me twenty-one years ago. Except you haven't had your happy ending yet. But don't lose hope, sweetheart. You can stay here for as long as you like. For as long as it takes.'

'For as long as what takes? For me to get over Mack? Or for me to change and become the woman I want to be?'

'Well yes. For all of that. But more importantly, for Ward and you to fall in love. You've taken the first steps, but there're a few hurdles you both need to overcome, and they may take time.'

'Fall in love with Ward! Why would I want to do that? And there's no chance of him falling in love with me. He made that clear today when he told me what he thinks of me. He's just keen to get me into bed, like all the men I meet. They only want me for sex, not for a permanent relationship. I'm not wife-material. And I'm certainly not the motherly type. There is no way Ward would even consider me as a replacement for his dead wife.'

Tracy tuts. 'Sometimes you do say the most dreadful things, Geneva. I hope he never does see you as a replacement for his dead wife! No woman should ever be a replacement for another. Dead or alive. Ward must want you because he loves you. And he must love you for your flaws as well as all the good qualities you have. You're not the only woman with flaws, sweetheart. We all have them. Some people are simply better at hiding them than others. Some never admit to having them. But we're not interested in others right now. The only people we're concerned with are you and Ward.'

'There is no, me and Ward. And I don't want there to be. I've got a fantastic life. I don't need him. I don't want him. I just need to be a better person so that I am happy with myself. I want to treat people as they should be treated; as I want them to treat me. I want to consider others, and not be so selfish. If I can achieve that, I'll be happy. The truth is, I don't want to turn into Mum and Dad. I realise that's a horrid thing to say about my parents – but it's true. And one thing my long relationship with Mack has taught me is that you can't force someone to love you. Even if I did have feelings for Ward – which I don't – I can't force him to have those same feelings for me. Unrequited love is no picnic, believe me. That's a path I don't want to wander down again.'

'I'm not suggesting you can force someone to love you, sweetheart. But you won't have to try to force Ward. You see, I know him. And I knew his wife. He's not looking for a replacement for her. He's not even looking for love. And yes, he probably was hoping for a fling with you. The man has eyes, and as you say yourself, most men want you. Ward is no different on that score. But he is different in many other ways. He's been exceedingly careful not to get involved with anyone. He won't want to risk losing someone he loves, again. And he won't do anything that might risk making Eve unhappy. She is the only person who really matters to him now. But from the things you've told me he said, and his behaviour towards you, I'd say you've woken something in that heart of his and it's taken him by surprise. He doesn't know what to do, and he clearly doesn't know what to say or how to say. Although he did seem to open up far more than I would have expected him to, so that in itself means there's hope.'

'Hope? Hope for what?'

'For love, of course!' She beams at me. 'The other things Ward cares about are this island and the people who live here, and of course, the ferry, and keeping that business afloat. Excuse the pun. He also cherishes Locke Keep. It's been in his family for centuries. Since it was built in 1070, only it was wood back then. The present Keep was built in 1370. The place has stood for all these years, and not only has it been a fortress, it's also been the family home. It's been deteriorating ever since, and being on an island with little protection from the elements doesn't help. When the Lockes owned every inch of the island and all the buildings on it, there was money coming in by way of rents. When funds ran short, mortgages could be taken out against the properties. Since Ward's grandfather and father started selling off land and buildings so that islanders could own their own homes, including Roger owning this cottage, cash to fill the Locke family chest has no doubt been in short supply. No rents, and fewer properties on which to arrange a mortgage. Ward wants to bring more visitors here, and to bolster the income of every business, and every resident. So he'll be careful who he falls in love with. It'll have to be someone who wants to live on Locke Isle, because he'll never leave this place. Not even for love. His wife hoped he would, despite the fact he had made it clear from the start, that leaving here wasn't an option for him, and it never would be.'

'His wife wanted to leave?'

Everything that Tracy had just told me was the same or remarkably similar to what Ward had told me himself. But he hadn't told me that his wife had wanted to leave Locke Isle. He hadn't said anything about her other than that she was dead.

'Yes. She was born in Folkestone and although she loved Ward, she never really loved the island. Ward did everything he could to make her see how good things could be here for her. For all three of them. But in the end, she wanted to go. There was talk of a trial separation. She said she was happy for Eve to remain with Ward. Then she suddenly fell ill and was diagnosed with terminal cancer and was dead within a matter of months. That was a terrible time for Ward and, of course, for her. Thankfully, Eve was so young she didn't fully understand. She was just two when her mum passed away. That was six years ago and Ward hasn't been close to anyone since. Not romantically. And that's how I know he has feelings for you, even though he may not realise quite what they are, himself, just as you say you don't have feelings for him.'

'I don't. I don't think. How do you know him so well? I realise this is an island and it's not exactly large, but does he open up to everyone here, or is it because you are you?' I smile at her. 'You always knew how to extract the truth from everyone.'

She smiles. 'It's partly that, but it's mainly because I'm Roger's wife. Ward's father and Roger were close friends, believe it or not, and Ward has always spent time here with us, or out on the ferry with Roger. He doesn't speak so frankly and honestly to others, but he has always opened up to us. He does keep some things to himself, of course, but I know him well. And possibly, as in a situation such as this, better than he knows himself. I'll tell you how I know he feels something for you. He held your hair while you were sick. He minded your luggage while you shopped. He bought you roses, and he held your hand. He even asked to see you again. And then, from the bits and pieces you remember and have told me about your 'argument', Ward said he felt something today he hadn't felt for many years. He even said he didn't believe in love at first sight but that for a moment today – and then you said he stopped. That's when he dismissed what he felt, as him merely being blown away by your looks. I would say he's already half in love with you.'

'Half in love with me? No. You're wrong. A man in love – even half in love, wouldn't say the horrid things he said. Not that I know what a man in love would say. I've never had a man in love with me before.'

'Until now.' She pats me on my knee. 'But another thing I know about Ward, is that he'll fight against his feelings. He knows about your life, Geneva. He knows how wealthy you are. The last thing he will want is for you, and for others, to think he's after your money. And he won't believe you'd want to stay on this island. Or that you'd want to be any sort of a mother to Eve. You have a jet-set lifestyle, a successful career, fame, and fortune, and, in his mind, not a care in the world. He has a young daughter he adores, several businesses all of which are struggling financially, a Keep that's crumbling around his ears, people he feels responsible for, whether he should or not, and he's juggling so many things that he doesn't have time for himself or for love. Those are the hurdles you'll both need to jump. But it's up to the two of you to decide whether you want to jump them.'

'We've only just met,' I protest. 'Besides, love shouldn't be so difficult, should it? Look at you and Roger. Everything simply fell into place.'

She nods. 'That's true. It did. But it hasn't always been smooth sailing. We've hit a few gales and rough seas over the years, but we've weathered them because we love one another and we've found our tranquil waters together.'

I grin at her. 'I can tell you're in love with a ferryman. Or former ferryman I suppose I should say. All those references to wind and water.'

Tracy laughs. 'Ah yes. Once a ferryman, always a ferryman, so Roger says. And remember, sweetheart, my darling Roger and I met on that ferry, in a similar fashion to you and Ward, and we've been together for just over twenty years. Love comes to us when we least expect it, and often when we don't want it. Or when we think we don't. If it's meant to be, it will be, but sometimes it demands something from us in return. I don't believe love should be easy. Sometimes it is and sometimes it isn't. What matters is how hard you are prepared to work when things get tough. I believe the harder you work, the better love becomes. Now shall we go and join Roger at the Watershed? We bought a few bottles of champagne, so I'll grab one from the fridge. According to the papers, that's the only thing Geneva McBriar will drink.'

She winks at me as we stand up. I link my arm through hers and we walk towards the kitchen.

'Is that what they say? I try not to read the articles about me because they're not always truthful. In this case, for example, champagne isn't the only thing I will drink. I've had several cups of coffee today, and just this afternoon, I drank an entire bottle of water! And let's not forget, I've also had a brandy. You see. You can't believe everything you read in the papers.'

Ten

The evening air is surprisingly balmy in the garden. The grass smells freshly cut, and vies for attention with scents of lavender, rosemary, and other herbs, along with several fragrant flowers. Even the sea air finds its way to my nostrils, but then again, the garden is near the edge of a cliff, sitting on a small island surrounded by salt water.

I can't help but smile when I see the Watershed. It looks exactly how I had pictured it from Tracy and Roger's earlier descriptions. The red, white, and blue bunting flutters in the warm breeze and although it isn't dark yet, the fairy lights are already twinkling, as are the battery-operated candles.

Roger looks relaxed lounging in one of a set of reclining, garden chairs with integrated footrests. There's a matching dining table, sofa and two side tables. The padded cushions are a plain, but pleasant grey, but I can't help thinking that they should be red, white, and blue to match the bar itself, and the bunting. I could have some made for them.

And that reminds me that I haven't given him and Tracy the rest of their gifts. I bought handmade chocolates, some heavenly-scented soaps, an ornately crafted candle, two watercolours of the Harbour Arm, one as it was in its heyday of steam packets to France, and one as it is now. I know that this bar folds up, but the watercolours might be right at home here.

'I have a few gifts for you,' I say, as Tracy hands Roger the champagne and asks him to do the honours.

'Gifts?' Tracy says, looking not all together pleased. 'I told you, Geneva, we don't need gifts. But it's lovely of you, of course.'

I smile at her. 'You don't know what they are yet. And they're only small. I bought them in Folkestone at the Marketplace. I'll nip inside and get them if you'll tell me the way to my room, please.'

'I'll show you,' Tracy says.

'No need. You sit and relax. I'm sure I can find it. Left or right at the top of the stairs?'

'First door on the left,' says Roger. 'We

thought you'd like a sea view. I won't pop this cork till you're back. Don't want the bubbles going flat.'

'Or the room at the back on the right is free, if you prefer a view of Locke Keep.' Tracy winks mischievously.

I grin at her. 'The sea view sounds perfect, thank you. I won't be long.'

I hurry inside and up the stairs, wondering if they're slightly slanted or if it's me, but when I reach the top and look back down, and it's definitely the stairs.

Is this old settlement from the hundred or so years this cottage has been here? Or is this a more recent shift in the land on which the cottage sits? Is it subsidence, or worse? Tracy said Roger owns this cottage. I assume it's insured, but what about against coastal erosion? Not all homes can be, I'm aware of that. And some home owners whose homes have succumbed and fallen over the cliffs, or are about to fall, even have to pay to have their homes demolished while still repaying their mortgage.

I mustn't interfere. This is their home, and Ward Locke's island. I'm certain their combined efforts will ensure White Cliffs Cottage won't disappear over the edge one night. The other cottage I saw on the opposite cliff will go first. Not that that thought is any comfort. Especially not to the owners of that cottage.

I couldn't bear it if Tracy and Roger lost their home. There must be something I can do. I'll have to make discreet enquiries. And, I suppose, I'll have to have a quiet word with Ward.

I dismiss all such thoughts from my head for now. This is a happy reunion. I find the shopping bags containing the gifts and I dash down the slanting stairs and back out into the garden.

Roger pops the champagne cork the moment I step outside, and fills the beautiful champagne saucers Tracy has set out on the table. We all clink glasses and say, 'Cheers.'

'To you, Geneva McBriar,' Tracy says, holding her glass in the air after that first sip. 'And to the exceedingly beautiful woman you have become. And to the even more beautiful woman you soon will be.'

'Thank you,' I say. 'And here's to the kindest, most caring and loving, and also the most beautiful, both inside and out, woman I've ever known, and to your extremely handsome husband.'

'I'll drink to that!' Roger says, laughing. 'It's my turn, isn't it?' He studies me for a moment and then he smiles. 'To finding love on a ferry. Or on an island. Or wherever it may be. To love. To us. And to the future.'

'I'll drink to that.' I smile as I repeat his

words.

How much has Tracy told him? I don't mind, of course, providing he doesn't repeat any of it back to Ward. I'd hate that man to know I arrived here in tears, and spent the first hour telling Tracy all my woes.

'Oh. Your presents!' I hand them the bags, and then I finally sit on one of the reclining chairs. It's far more comfortable than I expected, and I kick off my sandals and relax. 'They're all joint presents, because, I'm ashamed to say, I wasn't sure what you might like.'

'You open them, darling,' Roger says, quirking an eyebrow in a teasing fashion. And then he smiles at me. 'I don't even open my own birthday or Christmas presents, unless I get to them before my darling wife. No present is safe with Tracy in the house.'

'I can't help it,' she says, unwrapping the tissue paper from the candle. 'I like opening presents. And you open them far too slowly for me. I need to see what's inside.'

'Even the ones she's bought,' he tells me.

'I can't always remember what they are,' she says. 'Oh darling, look at this! Isn't it gorgeous? And the smell. It's divine.' Tracy passes the candle to him and he takes a long sniff.

'Oh that is,' he says. 'That needs to go beside our bed, don't you think?'

Tracy nods but she's already diving into the next one. It is one of the watercolours and both she and Roger exclaim in delight.

'I didn't know about the Watershed when I bought them,' I say, 'but it occurred to me just now that they might look good in here.'

'They would,' says Roger. 'But I think they may be too nice for here. The Watershed isn't always that watertight.'

'We could take them in when it rains,' Tracy suggests, looking at me as if seeking my approval.

'They're yours, so you should put them wherever you want them to be.'

'What about in the sitting room?' Roger says. 'Then we can remember this visit every time we look at them.'

'That's perfect,' says Tracy, peering into the next bag. 'Handmade chocolates! Oh, Geneva. These are so expensive. Everything here is. You really shouldn't have done this. Thank you so much. We will treasure them all. But we'll eat the chocolates now. Oh goodness!' She suddenly looks horrified. 'I haven't asked if you've eaten! And bearing in mind you told me that you left Ward and Eve ordering pizza at the café, I rather think you haven't! What must you think of me?'

I hadn't realised I'd hadn't eaten since lunch, either. And yet I'm not at all hungry.

'I think you're a wonderful woman. And one who shouldn't worry. I'm not hungry. Truly I'm not. But I will have just one of those chocolates, if I may, because they do look rather delicious.'

'Have as many as you like,' says Tracy. 'Are you sure you're not hungry? What about a sandwich? Or cheese and biscuits? But have some chocolates first.' She holds the box towards me and I take one. 'Don't tell me you need to maintain your figure,' she adds, tutting for effect.

'I won't. And I don't.' I laugh. 'This is simply because I'm just not hungry, but I can't resist temptation.'

'You are so kind,' Roger says, taking three when Tracy passes the box to him.

'You're naughty,' says Tracy, also helping herself to three.

The chocolates are going down a treat, as is the champagne, and I decide now is as good a time as any.

'Erm. There's something I want to discuss with you both, and I think it's best if we do that right now. Don't worry. It's nothing bad. But please don't be cross and don't be offended. I want to pay you for letting me stay here.'

'No!' Tracy snaps.

'Absolutely not,' says Roger, somewhat crossly.

'But I want to!'

'And we won't accept that,' Tracy sticks out her chin, and Roger nods.

I sigh loudly and dramatically. 'In that case, I'll have to ask Ward to take me back to the mainland tomorrow, which is such a shame as I think I would like it here.'

'What?' Tracy shrieks. 'You've only just arrived.'

'I thought you planned to stay for several weeks?' queries Roger.

'Plans change. If I'd gone to Fiji or somewhere, I would've paid to stay there. I suppose I could stay at Castle Keep Hotel. I'm sure they'd be only too happy to take my money.'

'If ... if you don't want to stay here and would rather stay at the hotel,' Tracy says, 'we completely understand. This cottage isn't to everybody's taste.'

'No! That's not what I meant at all. I told you not to be offended.' I reach out and squeeze Tracy's hand. 'I want to stay here. Honestly I do. As long as I'm not in your way, of course. If and when I am, feel free to tell me. I mean that. But I won't stay here unless you allow me to at least pay my way.'

'You're our guest. And our friend. We don't want payment.' Tracy still looks hurt.

'And that means more to me than you can possibly imagine. But let's get real here for a second. I'm also a multi-millionairess. And I do mean, multi. I'm not trying to be rude, or to hurt or offend you, but this is important to me. Really important. I told you on the phone, when you first made your kind offer, that I would pay my way. I meant it then, and I mean it now. I want to contribute in some way. I'm not suggesting a nightly rate, or anything. That would make us all feel as though this were a B and B, and it's not. I just want you to allow me to contribute financially. Look. I'll type into my phone what it would cost me to stay at my favourite hotel for one week. This is not a hotel and I do want to help out and do my share, so let's halve that weekly rate. Will you *please* accept that?'

Tracy's mouth falls open and Roger looks as if he may fall off his chair when I show them the screen.

'You ... you pay that for one week!' Tracy's voice is shrill.

'No. This is half of that, remember?'

'For one week?' Roger repeats, and then gulps down his champagne as if he's in total shock.

'Yes. Are we agreed? Or should I call Castle Keep Hotel for a room?'

Roger tuts crossly, and then he looks at Tracy. 'Call the hotel.'

'No!' Tracy shrieks again, sounding as

surprised as I feel. I really thought they would accept.

'Let me finish,' says Roger. 'You're clearly stubborn. I accept that. And you obviously feel strongly about this. Nothing wrong with that. You and my darling wife meant a great deal to one another many years ago and there has always been a bond between you. I love that. So this is what I suggest. Call Castle Keep Hotel and find out the cost of a room there for one week. Whatever that cost is, halve it, and we will accept that. We still won't be totally happy about it because you are our guest whatever you may say, but life is about compromise. Do we agree?'

'I'm happy with that,' I say, relieved.

'I ... I suppose so,' says Tracy, reluctantly.

'Excellent! And we don't need to call as I won't be booking a room. We can search online and find the cost.'

Now I'm the one whose mouth drops open and whose eyes bulge, but not because the hotel is expensive, but because it is such a bargain. I find the most luxurious suite, which is exactly what I would do if I intended to be a guest there, and then I show Tracy and Roger the total price for one week including breakfast and dinner.

'And remember,' I say, when I show

them, 'this doesn't include extras like the brandy and champagne I had last night, or anything like that, so I'll still be getting a really good deal.'

They both shake their heads as if they can't comprehend how I could think that was the case.

'This still doesn't feel right,' says Tracy.

'Staying here for free wouldn't feel right to me,' I say.

'We can buy more champagne,' says Roger, with a twinkle in his eyes, 'so we'll be giving Geneva some of her money back in liquid form.'

We all laugh at that.

'Absolutely,' I say. 'Because we all know that Geneva McBriar will only drink champagne!'

Eleven

Roger was right about the stars. There were thousands of them last night.

Okay, I know that's a drastic understatement. What I mean is, there seemed to be thousands visible to the naked eye last night, once it eventually grew dark.

We sat outside until late and by the time I fell into bed, after insisting Tracy and Roger take the money we had agreed on earlier, it was almost midnight. They couldn't believe that, not only was I prepared to pay them what they saw as a considerable sum of money, I had several times that amount with me in cash.

'I like to be prepared,' I had said. Although I don't usually carry substantial amounts of cash around. In fact I rarely carry cash at all. But this was an entirely new experience for me and I didn't know how much I might need.

Having got that slightly awkward situation out of the way, I slept like a baby and woke to the sounds of the sea and to gulls calling overhead.

It takes me a moment or two to remember where I am, but now that I have, I feel oddly at home.

The bed is comfortable and the bedroom is cosy, with its pale yellow walls, and pictures dotted here and there. There's an oak wardrobe, a chest of drawers, a small dressing table and stool, a tiny fireplace, currently filled with a vase of dried flowers and what looks like ... driftwood, and a bedside table on which there's a small vase brimming with fresh flowers, clearly picked from the garden.

No interior designer has set foot in White Cliffs Cottage, and yet the ambiance this place exudes is far more welcoming than many of the luxury hotels in which I've stayed.

The sun is shining through the pale yellow curtains, birds are singing, and the delightful aroma of freshly brewing coffee is trailing up those slanting stairs.

I get out of the comfy bed and stroll over to the window, drawing the curtains back too quickly and almost blinding myself with the light. I open the sash window and lean out, resting my elbows on the frame, and I breathe in the salt air. I could get used to this. The sea is the bluest azure, and as calm and flat as a mirror, reflecting the matching blue of the cloudless sky.

Folkestone and the Harbour Arm, together with a stretch of the Kent coast, and especially the white cliffs of Dover, are all clearly visible from my window. I can see Dover Castle, and the ferry port; there's a large ferry arriving, and I can see towns and homes and countryside. It all seems so far away and yet so near. And then my eyes spot the Locke Isle ferry, moored alongside Boardwalk, and I immediately think of Ward.

I quickly move away from the window, closing it behind me and shutting out the light with the curtains. I will not let him ruin my good mood.

Tracy told me last night that she and Roger are early risers, and it's not just the aroma of fresh coffee that is wafting towards me now. Bacon, toast, and other smells of a cooked breakfast tease me.

I grab my things and hurry to the bathroom next door to my bedroom. En-suites aren't a thing in White Cliffs Cottage, so I've been told, but it does have two bathrooms which is apparently unusual for a home of this size.

Again, this is not what I am accustomed

to, but then the whole point of this ... adventure is to experience new things, and to see life from other people's perspective. While not luxurious, the bathroom is more than adequate. Thankfully there is a shower.

Ten minutes later, with my long hair still damp and tied into a loose bun, my face free of make-up, and wearing jeans and a T-shirt, I make my way down those slanting stairs to find Tracy and Roger busy in the kitchen.

'Good morning,' I say, ridiculously pleased to see them. 'Something smells wonderful. Is there anything I can do to help?'

'Good morning,' they reply in unison.

'Did you sleep well?' Tracy asks.

'Incredibly so, thank you. Did you?'

'We did, sweetheart. Thanks for asking. And no, there's nothing you can do, except sit at that table and make yourself at home. Roger is making us his best, English breakfast. Coffee?'

'Yes please.'

I sit at the kitchen table and watch as they go about their tasks. Roger is softly humming along with a tune I don't recognise that is playing on an old fashioned radio, while placing bacon, sausages, mushrooms, tomatoes, and eggs on a plate; Tracy pours me coffee and hands me the large mug.

'Thanks for this. I could smell it from my

bedroom.'

Tracy nods. 'That's the only problem with homes like this. You can smell every smell and hear every sound. I hope we didn't disturb you when we got up.'

'No! And that's not what I meant. I meant it smelt heavenly. As for noise. I didn't hear a thing. Apart from the gulls this morning and then the birdsong, which was lovely. And the fresh sea air was a wonderful treat to wake up to.'

She smiles appreciatively as if I've set her mind at rest. Roger places a plate before me, piled high with food, and I realise I'm ravenous.

'The plate is hot, so be careful. I hope you enjoy this.'

'I have no doubt I shall. Thank you. It looks and smells delicious.'

Unlike at my parents' house, or even at my own home when Mack was with me, breakfast at this table is a loud and amusing experience. Both Tracy and Roger sing along to snippets of various songs on the radio from time to time, and they butter each other's toast, steal food from one another's plates, and generally fool around. Dad would be furious; Mum would be appalled. I'm not sure what to make of it but I find myself smiling and laughing and when we have finished, I don't want it to end.

'It going to be a beautiful day,' Tracy says, getting up from the table.

'Do you have plans?' Roger asks me.

'Erm. No, I don't.' That is a first for me. 'Other than to help with these dishes.' That is also a first. I get up to help clear the plates but Tracy stops me.

'Oh no you don't,' she says, in a tone I remember her using when I was young and about to do something I shouldn't. 'You're our guest, and you're on holiday.'

I smile and shake my head. 'I'm not on holiday. I'm here to learn to be a better person. And I'd rather think of myself as a friend than a guest. Friends help one another, or so a wise young woman recently told me. Please let me help you. It would make me happy. Truly it would.'

'Of course you're a friend,' Tracy says. 'I understand you wanting to help, but we would rather you relax. At least for the first few days. Let's make a deal.'

I grin at her. 'You know I'm an expert at those.' Memories of recent events come flooding back. 'Although recently, not so much.' I dismiss those thoughts. 'Okay. What's the deal?'

'You have fun this weekend. Do things you haven't done since you were a child. Wander around the island. That won't take too long. Meet some more of the locals. Make a few friends of your own age. Although there aren't too many of those to choose from, but there'll also be day trippers from Folkestone, and holidaymakers from farther afield. I'll be looking after Eve for part of the day, so you're welcome to join us. Or if you'd rather not, that's fine.'

'Eve? Ward's daughter?' Eve had told me that Tracy looked after her so I don't know why I'm surprised.

'Yes. I've been her part time nanny since she was born, more so after her mother died. She attends a school in Folkestone on week days but if the weather is bad and the ferry can't cross, I tutor her at home.' Tracy hands the plates to Roger who stacks them in the dishwasher. 'She's off now for the school holidays, of course, and she spends most of her time with Ward or with Aggie. That's Ward's aunt. Her name is Agatha but everyone calls her Aggie.'

'The one who owns the store on Boardwalk?' I ask.

Tracy nods. 'That's the one. And the shop where you bought that pretty mac you were wearing last night.'

'The Clothing Locker? So the name is connected to the Lockes? I did wonder. I met a young woman in there, called Natalie.'

'Ah, Natalie,' Roger says, shaking his head. 'Lovely young lady, but unlucky in love.

Just like her mother. And her grandmother before her. Let's hope Natalie's daughter breaks that particular mould.'

'They've all had children outside of marriage,' Tracy says, and then whispers, 'Roger dated her mother for a while but things didn't work out.'

'No need to whisper,' Roger says with a smile. 'I don't have any secrets, as you well know.'

'Is Aggie a bit of a tyrant?' I ask.

'Aggie? No! Why would you think that, sweetheart?'

'Just something Natalie said yesterday. She made a bit of a faux pas and when she realised, she virtually begged me not to make a complaint, and said she needed the job.'

'Ah. I suppose Aggie would take a complaint seriously, and she might have a word with Natalie about it, but as for the girl losing her job? No. Aggie knows, as we all do, that the family is struggling financially.'

'Every family on the island is struggling financially,' says Roger. 'Including the Lockes. Although everyone in the world seems to be right now. Cost of living crisis, my foot. The entire world's gone mad.'

'Let's not dwell on that,' says Tracy, looking a tad embarrassed. 'It's a beautiful day. Let's enjoy it.'

'Right,' says Roger, his expression

sheepish, as if he's just remembered we made a cash transaction last night, and that I am definitely not struggling financially.

I could probably buy this island and everything on it, ten times over, and still have plenty of money to buy myself champagne.

Somehow, right now, that doesn't feel quite as good as it usually would.

'At what time will you be looking after Eve?' I ask, changing the subject.

'Aggie is having Eve this morning. The first ferry leaves Boardwalk at 8.45 a.m. so Ward will be dropping her off at Aggie's any minute. I'll be collecting Eve from Aggie around 3 p.m. this afternoon, and Ward will collect her from here on his way home this evening.'

'Oh, I see. I got the impression yesterday that they spent a lot of time together. Won't he be taking her with him on the ferry today? Or was yesterday unusual?'

Roger chuckles. 'That little miss wants to be a pirate, bless her. She'd spend all day and night on board that boat if she could. Ward often takes her with him, but the weekends are the busiest time for the ferry, and Ward likes to keep a close eye on her, naturally. He can't do that if he's also got a boat-full of passengers.'

'No. I suppose not. I'd like to join you this afternoon, but I'm not that good with

147

children.'

'Aren't you?' Tracy says, and there's a twinkle in her eye. 'That's odd. While you were in the shower this morning, Ward phoned, to confirm our plans still held good, and he asked if you might be around when I have Eve. Apparently, she was upset that you didn't say goodbye yesterday, and she wants to see you today. He said it was a struggle to stop her from calling here on their way home from the café after supper.' She chuckles. 'Although I don't think Eve was the only one who wanted to stop off here last night to see you again.'

'Ward phoned? This morning? And you're only telling me this now? Sorry. Why would you tell me? He was checking on his plans, that's all. I'm being ridiculous. Forgive me.'

'Nothing to forgive, sweetheart.' Tracy pats my hand and smiles at Roger. 'I must say though, you seem rather flustered over a trifling phone call from a man you say you have no feelings for.'

'I...' I'm about to make a facetious remark but then I realise that's the old me. The new me can accept some teasing from a friend. A friend who seems to know me better than I know myself. 'How was he? Did he ... did he seem annoyed? Concerned? Not really bothered?'

'Oh he's bothered,' Roger says, chuckling. 'He's definitely bothered. Right. I must be off. Locke Isle Tourist Office won't open by itself.'

'Locke Isle...? You ... you work at the tourist office on Boardwalk? I thought you were a retired ferryman?'

'I am. Now I work part time at the tourist office, and join Ward on the occasional ferry sailing.'

He kisses Tracy on the lips, smiles at me and pats my hand, picks up a flask of something, and strides towards the front door, waving as he goes.

'Does he get paid for that?'

Tracy expresses her surprise at my blunt question by quirking an eyebrow but then she smiles.

'Ward tries to pay him, but Roger does it because he wants to, so Ward finds other ways to recompense him for his time. And yes, before you ask, Ward does pay me for looking after Eve, and I take it because, like you, Ward is as stubborn as a mule. But so is Roger. The only reason he agreed to your offer last night was because he knew you meant well, and how important it was to you. And also because he knew that you have far more money than Ward and the Lockes ever did, or ever will have.'

'How bad are things for Ward

financially, do you know?'

'No. No one does. Not even Aggie, his aunt. He's struggling, obviously. But he and Aggie always manage to pay their staff on time, he keeps the ferry running and all the other businesses in which he's involved, afloat. And he's generous to those who are in serious need.'

'He still owns other businesses on the island?'

'Yes. Aggie owns the store on Boardwalk and the one on Main Road. Ward either still owns, or still has a part share in most of the other businesses here. Not everyone could afford to buy their own businesses from his father, grandfather or from Ward, so he is selling those businesses to each business owner or owners, bit by bit. Like White Cliffs Café, for example. He still has a share in that.'

So is that why we went there? I can't help but wonder. Perhaps Ward doesn't have to pay, even though he said he had.

'And the florist's?'

'No. Bernie's husband was able to buy that via a mortgage which was paid off when he passed away.'

'Does that mean Ward gets free meals at the café?'

'Good heavens, no! Ward is like his father and grandfather. You don't take money out of a business until it's making good profits year on year. And the café will never do that. It just about breaks even after Sylvie and Cece are paid.'

'What else does Ward still own?'

The pub, The Beacon Inn, but he leases it to Harry and June Flight. And he owns Castle Keep Hotel, of course, but Tristan Goldsby manages that.'

'Ward owns the pub and the hotel?' I'm astonished by that, for some reason. Having seen the room rates of the hotel, I have doubts about Ward's business acumen.

'Yes. He also owns Fifi's, the French restaurant I told you about yesterday. Oh, and the lighthouse.'

'So, basically, Ward still owns most of this island?'

'I suppose he does, and yet, it doesn't feel that way. Most of the homes here are owned by the occupants, or those that are still rented out, are long-term, so it seems as if they are owner-occupied even if they're not. I only know so much about it because of the things Ward and his dad, told Roger, and I'm also a close friend of Aggie's, and over the years, she has told me a lot more than she probably should have. I'm not sure how many other people on the island know about his financial situation, but every islander knows that Ward wants each and every one of us to not only own our own homes, but also the businesses we run.'

'Perhaps that's part of the problem. From what you've told me, he seems so intent on everyone owning their home or business, that he's less concerned about profits. He may find one day that everyone on this island owns their own home, apart from him, because he'll have mortgaged Locke Keep to the hilt to cover everyone else's costs. Perhaps he should spend more time ensuring his businesses make money. He could increase the hotel room rates, for one thing.'

'The hotel is half empty, so he won't do that,' Tracy says. 'And he could increase rents, but I happen to know he hasn't done that either, and he won't. He's thinking of all sorts of ways to get more tourists here and to find other income streams to help the residents and businesses, but as Roger said last night, times are tough for many people right now. This is an island and it's small, so big businesses aren't interested in investing. Some have made him offers for the land, the hotel, and for the Keep, but he'll never sell. It sounds dramatic I know, but he would honestly die first. Having said that, if he had to sell everything to save Eve's life or something, he would do that in a second.'

'Why won't he sell the hotel, at least?

Even Dad would be interested in that.'

'I think you've answered your own question. Ward loves this island, and while he wants it to be profitable, he also wants it to be a place where the islanders who are born and bred here, can afford to live. The last thing he wants is for prices to sky-rocket. If someone like your dad got his hands on the hotel, do you honestly think the island would remain the same?'

'No. It definitely would not.' I have to concede that point. The man is either a saint or a fool. I can't quite make my mind up. And he's far too generous and considerate of others, for his own good.'

'Isn't that what you've said you want to be?'

I laugh at that. 'Yes. But not to that extreme. I still want to be rich. Ward sounds too good to be true.'

And yet, I know from personal experience, that the man is very, very real.

Twelve

I can't stop thinking about Ward, as I head off for a walk around Locke Isle.

But at least I'm no longer thinking about Mack. Apart from now, of course.

The person I should be thinking about, is me.

Or is it? Aren't I supposed to be thinking of others?

I laugh at the insanity of this situation.

I want to be a better person, but I don't want to be as good as Ward seems to be.

I want to consider others, but not to the extent that I put those others too far ahead of myself.

I want to help, but I don't know where to start.

At least I spent the past few hours helping Tracy with household chores. Again, not something I would ever do myself, but once I knew what to do and how to do each one, it wasn't that bad.

I won't be letting any of my own staff go though. Apart from the fact that I have more profitable ways of spending every hour of every day, after a couple of hours wearing rubber gloves, I've decided it's not a good look on me. I'll still help Tracy while I'm here, but when I return to my own world, those gloves will not be going with me.

From White Cliffs Cottage, I cross Main Road on to Lighthouse Way. I consider walking along the shore to the lighthouse but the only road down to the beach leads directly on to Boardwalk and I don't want to risk seeing Ward.

This road skirts the boundary of Locke Keep and from here I get another perspective of the ancient building. From the outside, it's a beautiful place. Imposing, magnificent, and magical. A lot like the owner, himself.

I desperately wish I could see inside – both the building and the man. But I've blown my chances on both scores, so I drag my gaze from the Keep and concentrate on the road ahead.

I hurry past Ferry Lane. I think I can guess where that might take me, and I definitely don't want to go there. The next on my left is Sands Way, which might lead down to the beach, yet something inside tells me to stay on the path I have chosen.

I wonder if the universe is trying to tell me something, and I smile as I walk on.

Now I can see the road splits at a sort of T-junction. To the right it appears to lead to one house, so I assume I need to turn left, but just as I am about to do so, I hear a door open and close, and someone calls my name.

'Gen! Gen! Wait for us.'

I recognise the voice immediately and I wait while the child runs to me, followed closely by the black Labrador.

'Morning, Captain Eve,' I salute. 'And hello second mate, Horatio. How are you today?'

'Cross,' says Eve, folding her arms in front of her chest to emphasize the point.

'With me?'

'Yes.'

'Because I left without saying goodbye?'

'Uh-huh.'

I bend down so that we are at eye level and I place my hands on her arms.

'I'm sorry I did that. It was rude and childish, and I should know better. Forgive me?'

If anyone had told me, even a week ago, that I would be apologising to an eight-year-old child, I would've told them they were insane. Yet here I am doing precisely that. And the odd thing is, I genuinely care.

'Why did you leave? We had pizza and

milkshake! Dad said he told you, you could stay.'

'He did. And pizza and milkshake sounded divine. The thing is, I am staying with friends and I was already late. And that was rude of me too. But I should've come and said goodbye to you and to Horatio, and not just left. I promise it won't happen again.'

'Dad said you were cross with him.'

'Did he? Well maybe I was, just a little.'

'Why?'

'Grown up stuff.'

'I'm grown up!'

'I know. But it was silly, and I'd rather not say. Would you mind if we forgot about it? I shouldn't have just left. I'm sorry. Please, please forgive me.'

She shrugs her shoulders high until they almost touch her ears.

'Okay,' she says. 'You're forgiven. Are you still cross with Dad?'

'No. I don't think so. But he may be cross with me.'

She shakes her curls. 'Na-uh. He said he hopes he'll see you again.'

'Did he!' That is a surprise. 'When did he say that?'

'Last night. I wanted to come to Nanny Tracy's but Dad said we had to go home and that he hoped we would see you tomorrow. And that's today. And I have seen you. But

Dad hasn't. Come and meet Aunt Aggie.' She grabs my hand and pulls me forward.

'Aunt Aggie?' Does she mean Ward's aunt?

'Eve!' There's a woman standing in the doorway of the house to the right. The one the road leads to. She has her hands on her hips and she's tall, slim and attractive, with the same curls as Eve and Ward, but hers are tied loosely in a knot. I would say she's in her late fifties but it's difficult to tell from here. I can tell she isn't pleased, though. She's wearing a long, floral patterned skirt, a white blouse and she has bare feet. 'I've told you before, don't go running out of the house and slamming the front door without telling me where you're going. Who's this?'

'Sorry about the door,' says Eve. 'But I wasn't going anywhere, that's why I didn't tell you. This is Gen. The pretty lady from the ferry.'

'Hi,' I say, giving her a small wave with my free hand.

'So you're Gen with a G, are you?'

She looks me up and down and I wonder what Ward has told her. Or maybe it was someone else. Someone from the café, perhaps. Eventually she smiles.

'I was making a pot of tea. Would you like a cup?'

'I would. Thank you. But I don't want to

disturb you.'

'You haven't. Ward on the other hand...' She tuts. 'That's another matter. I'm Aggie, Ward's aunt. Come in.'

Eve beams up at me, let's go of my hand and rushes back inside with Horatio at her heels.

'Shoes!' Aggie yells after her, but Eve is long gone, and so is Horatio. Not that he has shoes.

'Should I take my shoes off?' I ask as I step on to the wooden floor of the hall.

'Why?' Aggie asks, giving me an odd look over her shoulder.

'Erm. Because you've just told Eve to, and you're not wearing any.'

'Personal choice for me. I didn't tell Eve to remove her shoes. I merely reminded her to be careful. She has a tendency to slip and slide on these polished floors, mainly because she seems incapable of walking anywhere and needs to run everywhere she goes.'

Now I don't know what to do. Another first for me. I hesitate for a moment and Aggie turns and looks me up and down.

'Are you always this indecisive? From what Ward tells me you're a multi-millionairess who runs her own property portfolio and also jointly runs her father's property empire. Is that the problem? Do you have people who remove your shoes for you?'

Is she for real? Is she being serious, or winding me up? I really can't tell.

'I'll keep them on,' I say. 'And no. I don't have people to remove my shoes. Although clearly I need to add it to the long list of staff that I require to help me live my life.'

She bursts out laughing and turns and beams at me, walking backwards into her kitchen that opens out on to a beautifully manicured garden via a set of bi-fold doors. I spot Eve and Horatio playing on the grass, as Aggie wags one finger to and fro like a metronome.

'Now I see why Ward likes you.' Again her eyes scan me from head to toe. 'Apart from the obvious, of course. But Ward has never been one to be taken in by just beauty alone. With him there needs to be something more. Something deeper.'

'Ward told you he likes me?' Why does that make me feel so ridiculously happy?

She raises her brows, and she reminds me so much of Ward that a knot forms in my stomach.

'No. In fact he spent most of last night telling me just how much he *doesn't* like you.

'Oh.' The knot forms into a knife and it moves up towards my heart. 'That's fine. That's how I thought he felt.'

'Hmm,' she says, rolling her eyes. 'Eve,

on the other hand, has spent most of this morning so far telling me how great you are. And that was a surprise. Eve is very choosy about who she would have with her on her pirate ship, and you, it seems, have made the cut.'

'I have? That's as much of a surprise to me. I don't know anyone with children and I don't spend any time with them so I have no idea what they expect.'

'Hmm,' she says once again, and I'm grateful when Eve calls my name and orders me to join her and Horatio in the garden.

'Is it okay?' I ask Aggie.

'Go,' she says, waving one hand at me in a dismissive fashion. 'I'll bring the tea out to you. I'm sure you have staff who do that.'

I really can't tell if this is her idea of banter or not but I have a sudden urge to say something that would make the old Geneva proud. The problem is, I can't think of anything smart or sassy or even clever to say, so I hurry out to Eve and Horatio instead.

At least I feel at ease with them.

'Can you climb trees?' Eve asks.

'Oh! I've never climbed one. But I have climbed rocks and even a small mountain, so I think I could manage a tree. Except ... why would I want to?'

Eve gasps. 'You've climbed a mountain?'

'A small mountain, yes.'

'Did you stick a flag up at the top? I've seen people on TV do that.'

'Not a flag, no. A rock from the mountain. Climbers who reach the summit add to a pile of rocks and it was about your height, when I was there fifteen years ago. It might be much bigger now. You can trek up most of the mountain, it's only the last part that's harder.'

'Which mountain was it?'

'Mount Olympus, in Greece. The highest summit on the mountain is called Mytikas, and it's 2918 metres above sea level. I did it for charity.'

'Mount Olympus! That's where the gods lived!'

'That's right. But I didn't see any signs of them. Although they say the gods know you're there on the summit and they might answer you. I'm still waiting for that call.'

'Wait till I tell Dad!'

'Erm. I'm not sure your dad will be interested in something I did many years ago. But why did you ask about climbing trees?'

She points upwards with one forefinger and sticks the tip of her other forefinger in her mouth. It's strange how she seems so grown up one moment and so young the next.

'I tied Aunt Aggie's scarf to a balloon and

it got stuck in that tree.'

She's pointing to a large tree at the end of the garden and a burst of laughter escapes me although it isn't really funny.

'Why did you do that?'

Eve shrugs her shoulders high, just as she did earlier. 'I wanted to see how high it would go'

'Does Aggie know?'

Eve shakes her head.

'And will she be cross if you tell her?'

Eve nods. I sigh. Horatio makes a sort of sympathetic whimper.

'Then I suppose we have two choices. Either we stay quiet about it and pretend we don't know where it is if she asks. But that's not really the right thing to do. Is she likely to notice it's gone?'

Eve nods again. 'It's her favourite and she was wearing it last night.'

'Last night?'

'When she came over for a glass of wine and the banana bread Dad bought her.'

'So the banana bread yesterday was for Aggie?'

I wish I'd known that yesterday. I wish I'd known a lot of things yesterday.

'Uh-huh. It's her favourite. Just like the scarf.'

'I think I need to take a closer look.'

Eve takes my hand and leads me to the

tree; Horatio follows us. I can see the balloon and it's about twenty feet off the ground in the branches. I can also see why the 'scarf' is Aggie's favourite. Even from here I can see that the black scarf is actually a sheer silk stole, and probably expensive.

'You said two choices?' Eve reminds me.

'Yes. The second choice is that one of the three of us climbs up and gets it. I vote for Horatio.'

Eve laughs. 'He can't climb trees. And I can't reach the branches. Even on one of the garden chairs. I tried that earlier.'

'Earlier? How long has the balloon been in the tree?'

'An hour. That's how I saw you. I was looking out of the window for Jonas. He's the lighthouse keeper and he lives in Lookout Cottage at the end of Lookout Lane. He cycles to the store each day for a newspaper and then has breakfast in White Cliffs Café. I was waiting for him to come back.'

'I see. And why was that? Surely if you asked Jonas to come in and help, Aggie would find out what has happened?'

'Oh no. I wasn't going to ask Jonas in. I was going to ask him to climb over the garden fence and then climb up the tree.'

I can't help myself. This child has me in stitches.

'Right. Well I think we can leave Jonas in

peace. I'll climb the tree. You keep an eye out for Aggie. She was supposed to be bringing me a cup of tea. I think she may have forgotten.'

Either that or she has no intention of doing so, which seems odd, because she was the one who suggested it.

'You should hurry then,' says Eve.

I can reach the first branch without difficulty, thanks to my height, and I swing my legs up and then swing myself on to the branch. It's not really that different from a survival training program my personal fitness instructor devised for me to ensure I was getting an all over workout. I glance down at Eve and give her a thumbs up. She tells me to move faster.

I climb on to the branch above and then the next, but here it becomes more difficult. The tree is in full leaf and the balloon is stuck near the tips of the branches. It means I need to work my way outwards, away from the safety of the sturdy trunk and older branches and on to some of the younger, more twig-like ones.

'Are you there yet?' Eve calls up, trying to keep her voice low so that Aggie won't hear, no doubt.

'Not yet. The branches are thinner here.'

'Hurry! I can hear Aunt Aggie laughing.'

Eve would make a good pirate. She

would have no qualms forcing people to walk the plank.

I gingerly edge my way along a spindly branch and close my eyes as I hear a faint crack. I reach out my hand and grab for the stole and thankfully, I reach it. I quickly edge my way back with the stole stuffed safely down my T-shirt and then half swing, half leap from branch to branch, reminding me even more of my resemblance to a trained monkey.

'Got it!' I exclaim triumphantly when I swing myself down from the final branch and drop to the ground, pulling Aggie's beautiful sheer silk stole from my T-shirt along with the tattered remains of the balloon and the string they were both attached to.

'Who wants to explain?' Ward demands, looking as astonished as I feel. But also rather cross. Aggie is standing beside him, and she doesn't look pleased either. Even though I've retrieved her favourite stole. 'Well?' Ward adds. 'Whose bright idea was this?'

I look at Eve, and she looks at me, and then we both point at Horatio, who barks.

Thirteen

'Who is the adult here?' Ward snaps. He clearly didn't find it funny that Eve and I both pointed at Horatio.

The man is even more handsome and sexy when he's mad, but I shouldn't be thinking the things I am thinking.

'Oh come on,' I say, trying not to look at him. 'It's not the end of the world. Aggie's got her stole back, safe and sound. I don't have so much as a scratch on me. And the tree will soon recover.'

'Do you think this is funny?'

He's glaring at me now, but he has nothing on my dad, and I can't help but snigger.

'Honestly? Yes. A little. I wouldn't mind that cup of tea, please, Aggie. If it's still on offer.'

There's a twitch at the side of her mouth but she darts a look at Ward as if seeking his approval.

'Aggie, please take Eve inside.' Ward's voice sounds a bit like it did yesterday and I can tell I'm in for a lecture. Or worse. 'I want to have a word with Geneva.'

'I'm sorry, Gen,' Eve says. 'Please don't be cross with her, Dad. It was my fault.'

'Go with your aunt. I'll deal with you later.'

'But, Dad!'

'Go!'

'Come along, Eve,' says Aggie, taking her by the hand and almost dragging her away, but very gently.

Horatio follows, hanging his head. That dog is almost human.

I sigh. 'Save your breath, Ward. I know you're cross but you have no reason to be. What are you doing here anyway? Aren't you meant to be ferrying people back and forth all day?'

He raises his brows and he reminds me of a kettle full of steam, about to blow its lid. I clearly need that cup of tea.

Yet when Ward speaks again his voice is cold and hard.

'Cross doesn't even begin to cover the way I'm feeling right now. And yes. I am meant to be ferrying people back and forth, as you so deftly put it, but even ferrymen have to take a break. I came to see Eve, and to have lunch with my daughter and my aunt. It's either bad timing, or perfect timing depending on how you look at it. As for not having a reason to be cross, it obviously hasn't occurred to you for one second that my eight-year-old daughter has just watched you climb a tree with apparent ease and then swing yourself down in triumph. What sort of example do you think you've set?'

'Erm. That women can do anything?'

'I'm serious, Geneva!'

'So am I!'

'You could've killed yourself and landed in a crumbled heap at my ... at her feet!'

'But I didn't. And I was being careful. I'm not a complete idiot.'

'That's a matter of opinion. And the fact that she tied Aggie's stole to a balloon and sent it off without hope of return is perfectly acceptable to you?'

'No. But it has been returned, so there's no harm done. I agree you might need to have a word with her about taking other people's belongings without asking, but she is eight, and she was just experimenting.'

'Experimenting! And if she does something similar again and then remembers how easy it was for you, and climbs a tree and falls and breaks her neck, is that experimenting? Is that acceptable to you?' He is angry again.

'Of course not! But if you explain it to her properly, she won't do it again and she won't climb a tree because she'll know she mustn't. Believe me, if Dad told me not to do something again, I didn't. I didn't even contact my beloved nanny for twenty-six years because Dad told me not to. And I was Eve's age then. Not that I'm suggesting for a second that you should be like my dad, because I'm not. Oh, I don't know what I'm saying now because you're making me cross! Look! I know what you think of me. I know how much you dislike me, and if you tell me to stay away from Eve, I will. But she likes me and I'm sorry about that and I have no idea why she does, because I'm not a nice person, I'll admit. But I like her too and ... and ... Oh go to hell! I don't have to stand here and listen to you. I'm a grown woman and you have no control over me or what I do.'

I storm past, but he catches me by the arm and pulls me to his side, his eyes staring into mine with an intensity I've never seen before in any man's eyes and I don't understand, or recognise the look.

'And what if *you'd* fallen?' he growls, his face so close to mine that his breath on my cheek makes me tingle. 'What if you'd broken your neck? Why didn't you have the sense to call me?'

'I ... I ... I don't have your phone

number.'

'She wouldn't fall!' Eve yells, running towards us with Aggie chasing after her, and Horatio running after Eve. 'She climbed Mount Olympus and she reached the summit where the gods were!'

Ward blinks several times. 'What?'

I just know he is not going to believe that.

And I'm right.

He lets go of my arm so fast that I nearly stumble.

Great. I can climb a tree and a mountain but he lets me go and I can't stand on my own two feet!

'Now you're lying to her?' His voice is like ice and yet there's a hint of pain there. I recognise that sound from my own experiences.

'She didn't lie!' Eve shrieks.

I shake my head. 'Believe what you want, Ward. I really don't care anymore. Excuse me.'

I bend down to make eye contact with Eve. I see Ward move forward as if he's going to stop me and I also see Aggie put her hand on his arm to stop him.

'Your dad is understandably cross with me because I should have got Aggie to phone him and I shouldn't have climbed that tree. Even an experienced climber like me can fall.

I was lucky today, that's all. Promise me right now that you'll never climb a tree, or climb anything higher than a chair, unless there is an adult with you, like your dad, or an experienced climber, okay?'

'I promise.'

I hold out my little finger to her. 'Pirates' honour?'

She twists her little finger around mine. 'Pirates' honour.'

'Good girl, Eve. Now I've got to go.'

'No!' She shrieks.

'We'll still be friends,' I say, with no real idea of what I'm saying or doing, I'm so upset. 'I want to say goodbye to you and to Horatio for now, just in case I don't see you for a while.'

'Dad?' Eve looks up at him with tears in her eyes.

How did she get so attached to me so fast? And why?

But then again, how did I get so attached to her? And why? I really don't understand this at all.

'It's okay, Eve. I'll see you again, and that's a promise.'

I ruffle her hair as I stand up, smile wanly at Aggie, and pat Horatio on the head. I dare not look at Ward. I feel as if my heart is about to break, and I know that is ridiculous and I know it doesn't make sense, but I can't help feeling what I'm feeling.

'Bye then,' I say, and I blow Eve a kiss, and march off as fast as I can.

Fourteen

It is not easy to avoid someone when you are both stuck on an island that is only four miles or so long, and two and a half miles wide, but I am determined to manage it somehow.

The problem is, Tracy is supposed to be looking after Eve this afternoon, and Ward has probably forbidden Eve from seeing me ever again. Just like Dad did with Tracy when he considered her to be a bad influence on me. Although in this case, it is not because I might make Eve 'soft'. It is because I might make her take too many risks.

And the more I think about it – and I have done nothing but think about it for the last hour, I even have to accept that Ward might have a point. I get it. I really do. He obviously wants to keep his daughter safe.

I'm sitting near the edge of the cliff at the end of Sands Way, which does not lead to the beach after all, but ends abruptly, where I'm sitting. The cliff is high here, but I can see part of it tapers down towards the beach and if I really wanted to, I'm sure I could scramble down to the sandy shore below. Not that I want to. I've had enough adventure for one day.

People have no idea that there is this other side to me. I'd forgotten myself until now. Dad paid for my sailing lessons, climbing lessons, skiing lessons, archery, and fencing lessons, and all the other lessons he felt I should have. I might not have been a boy, but I could still do all the things he expected a son to do. Except shoot. I never have, and never shall have, any interest in shooting things, living, dead, or man-made. That was a disappointment to him, but one he forgave because I excelled at so many other things.

Mum, of course, paid for all the lessons she felt I needed to make me the perfect woman, or her idea of what the perfect woman should be. Which had nothing whatsoever to do with being a perfect wife or mother. She had no idea how to be either of those things herself. Not that I'm suggesting for one minute that a perfect woman has to be a wife and a mother. But it might be nice to at least have some notion of what that would entail. I'm not really sure why Mum married Dad. Nor why she had me.

That's why the way I feel about Eve is so surprising. I don't think I've ever really thought about having children. Until now. But there's something about Eve.

I suppose a part of that might be because I fancy her dad like crazy.

Yes. I still do, despite the things he said. Despite the fact he automatically assumed I'd lied about climbing Mount Olympus. If anything, after today, I fancy him even more. The way he looked at me when he grabbed my arm in Aggie's garden.

I quiver at the memory and wish he hadn't let go.

This is utter madness.

Now, instead of being grateful to Emma Barr for making me take that long, hard look at myself, I'm beginning to curse the thought of her. If not for her I'd be in my office in McBriar Tower right now, negotiating yet another deal to add to our multi-millions in the bank.

And yet, as I sit here staring out across the English Channel towards Folkestone, why is it that this place already feels more like home to me than any place I've ever been? How is that possible? I haven't even seen the rest of the island yet. I haven't even been here for twenty-four hours.

Perhaps home is less about a place and more about people. Tracy is here. We've been apart for years and yet she is more like a mum to me than Mum has ever been. And she's also a friend. My only real friend. But now I also have Roger as a friend. I liked him right away, and I feel at home in White Cliffs Cottage, despite its lack of en suite facilities.

And then there's Ward. And Eve. I had never been in love until I fell in love with Mack. But I know I could feel more for Ward and for Eve than I think I ever did for him. I already feel so much for them. It actually physically hurts just thinking that I might not see Ward or Eve again.

So much for being determined to avoid Ward.

And avoiding Ward is only half the battle. Tracy is Eve's nanny, and it is the school holidays. Eve will be spending a lot of time with Tracy. If Ward has decided that I must never see Eve again, I'll have to ensure I'm never at White Cliffs Cottage when Eve is there. I'll be so sad about that but I might not have a choice. The problem is, where can I go?

Ward owns shares in the café and is often there. He owns the hotel. He owns the only pub. He owns the French restaurant. I can't even get off the island because he owns and runs the ferry. Either he or his aunt own most of the businesses and shops on this island. There is literally, no getting away from the man.

Unless ... I can get off the island. All I need to do is make a call. And find somewhere for a helicopter to land. Or even a boat, other than the ferry, to come and get me from the Boardwalk. Once the ferry has stopped running for the day of course.

I don't want to get off the island though. And that is the real problem. But it's one that won't be solved by me sitting here and moping.

I'm here to change my ways and to learn to be considerate and helpful to others. Maybe if I concentrate on that, everything else will work itself out.

Fifteen

I head back to White Cliffs Cottage. I need to tell Tracy what has happened. I don't think Ward would have phoned her to change the arrangements, but it's only right that she hears my side of the story as well as his.

Tracy has given me a key so I let myself in. Roger has returned and they are both sitting in the garden at the table near the Watershed, eating lunch.

'Have you eaten?' Tracy asks the moment she sees me.

'Not since breakfast,' I reply.

'We're having bread and cheese,' she says. 'There's plenty of both if you fancy it. Or I can make you something else if you prefer.'

'Bread and cheese sound good. Don't get up. I'll help myself. May I make some tea? I've been gasping for a cup for ages.'

'Of course,' she says. 'Our home is your home. Are you sure I can't help?'

What she's really asking is, do I know my way around a kitchen and where to find the bread and cheese and how to make tea? Which of course I do.

'I'm fine thanks. Would you or Roger like a cup?'

'I wouldn't mind another,' Tracy says.

'Yes please,' says Roger.

I slice myself some bread and cheese, add a dollop of butter to my plate and take that, together with a tray on which I put a pot of tea, a jug of milk, a bowl of sugar and three cups and saucers, out to join them.

'I've got some news,' I say, placing the tray on the table. 'And it's not good, I'm afraid.'

'We know, sweetheart,' says Tracy, and she and her husband both give me a sympathetic smile.

'You know?' I drop into one of the reclining chairs. 'How? Did Ward call to tell you?'

'He mentioned it to me,' says Roger. 'He was on his way back to the ferry as I was closing up the tourist office to come home for lunch.'

'What did he tell you?'

Roger repeats what Ward had told him. Surprisingly, it's not that dissimilar to my version of events, the only real difference being that Ward still thinks I lied about

Mount Olympus.

'I didn't lie,' I say.

'We know,' Tracy says. 'Don't forget sweetheart, I've been following your progress over the years. As soon as Roger mentioned you'd said you'd climbed a mountain, I knew that was true because I'd not only read about it, I'd seen the photos of you and the rest of the team at the summit. It was for a children's hospital, if I remember correctly, and you and the others raised thousands of pounds.'

'We did.'

Tracy smiles. 'You see, Geneva. You say you need to change but you've always had the good you inside. It's just been pushed down so far that you've forgotten it's there.' She chuckles. 'I did laugh when Roger told me the part where both you and Eve pointed to Horatio. Of course, I completely understand why Ward was upset. But I am surprised, because the man has a good sense of humour. I would've thought he would have found that as funny as we did.'

Roger chuckles too, but then looks serious. 'I think Ward was so petrified that something dreadful could've happened that even though he knew you were both safe and sound he was still in panic mode and reacted accordingly.'

'He didn't sound panicked. He sounded

cool but annoyed, if that makes sense? And he could see Eve was safe and sound the second he walked into the garden.'

'Yes. But he couldn't see you. He told me he could hear rustling leaves and creaking branches and he almost had a heart attack when you landed right in front of him. It took him a moment or two before his heart would stop pounding and he realised you were standing safely on your feet and smiling as if nothing was wrong, when you could've easily fallen and killed yourself, and yet all you did was laugh and make jokes and blame the dog, as if you were an eight-year-old yourself.'

'Are you ... are you saying that he thought I'd fallen from the tree and hurt myself?'

Roger nods. 'Yes. Although the poor man was still so furious with you that he wasn't making a great deal of sense, even almost an hour after it happened.'

'Has he ... has he forbidden Eve from seeing me?'

'Good heavens, no!' Roger says. 'Why would he do that? It's obvious Eve likes you. He wants her to be happy. Besides, he's not that sort of man.'

'He's not like your dad, sweetheart,' Tracy says, hitting the nail on the head.

'Does that mean Eve will still be coming

here this afternoon? And that I can join you?'

'Of course she will. And yes. But we'd better make sure we all keep our feet firmly on the ground, just in case.' Tracy laughs.

I've just spent an hour worrying about nothing. I genuinely thought Ward would react like my dad had, but for entirely different reasons.

Tracy clears her throat. 'Is now a good time to mention that you seem to have part of an old birds' nest in your hair? I've only just spotted it.'

'What?' My hand shoots to my loose bun, which I now realise is a lot looser than it was, and I can feel some twigs, or something similar caught up in the clip I'd used to hold the bun in place. 'Excuse me, please.' I race inside and up the slanting stairs and I'm horrified by my reflection. Not only are there three small twigs sticking up at varying angles, but I'd forgotten I'm not wearing any make-up, and I've got a smudge of something on my cheek.

What a sight I look! Raymondo, my hairstylist, would be speechless with horror, and so would all the beauticians at my local, luxury spa.

What must Ward have thought seeing me like this? Quite a difference from yesterday, and the woman he'd wanted to take to bed. Today, I'm a complete mess.

I wash my face and brush my hair and try to tidy myself up, and then I see that I have managed to break a nail. I came to Locke Isle to change, but I didn't want to change into some sort of wild woman of the island.

Sixteen

'I'm sorry I got you into trouble,' Eve says, running to me and hugging my legs when Tracy brings her into the garden. Horatio shadows her, as always.

I smile at her and hug her back. 'Don't give it another thought. There's no harm done.' I stroke Horatio on the head, and he rolls over on the grass.

'You're not going to leave?' Eve pleads.

'No.'

'But you said you might not see us for a while?'

'I did, didn't I?' I take her hand and walk towards one of the reclining chairs. Horatio follows us and flops down under the table. Roger has gone back to the tourist office and Tracy is making a pot of tea for us, and a cold drink for Eve. 'I think that's because I was cross.'

'With me?'

185

I sit on the chair and lift her on to my lap. 'No, silly. With myself. I should've got Aggie to call your dad and I shouldn't have climbed that tree.'

'I asked you to.'

She fiddles with a lock of my hair that has once again fallen loose from my bun. I am clearly not as adept as Raymondo at being able to fix my hair firmly in place.

'Just because someone asks us to do something, it doesn't mean we have to do it. Not when we're grown-ups, at least. When we're young we should do what people tell us. Although ... not always.' I'm not particularly good at this. 'Erm. What I'm saying is that I should have said no, and I should have spoken to your dad about it. And you have remembered our promise, haven't you?'

She nods vigorously. 'I mustn't climb trees or anything higher than a chair unless Dad is with me, or someone experienced like you. But Dad told me I mustn't climb on to chairs either.'

'And he is right.'

'Do you ... like my dad?'

Where did that come from? I look her in the eye and she smiles sheepishly.

'Why did you ask that?'

She shrugs. 'I heard Aunt Aggie telling Dad that he's a fool, and that he needs to tell you.'

186

'Tell me? Tell me what?'

She shrugs again. 'I didn't hear that bit 'cos Horatio chased a squirrel and he's not supposed to do that, so I had to chase him and bring him back. But then Dad said, "Geneva McBriar has made it clear she doesn't like me." And you're Geneva McBriar, aren't you, Gen? I heard you say so on the ferry. Why are you called Geneva?'

'Erm. Because my mum liked the name. What else did your dad say?'

'Nothing. He saw me when Horatio barked and he told Aunt Aggie there was nothing else to say on the subject. So do you?'

'Do I what? Like your dad?'

'Uh-huh.'

I grin at her and nod. 'Uh-huh.' And then I hug her tight. 'But I don't think we should tell him.'

'Why not?'

'Because it's ... complicated grown-up stuff.'

She shifts a little to look me in the eye.

'But if Dad likes you, and you like Dad, and I like you, and you like me, and Horatio likes you, and you like him, isn't that nice?'

'It is. But sometimes nice doesn't work out.'

'Here's your orange juice, little one,' Tracy says carrying a tray into the garden.

'That's for me,' I joke.

'No,' says Eve scuttling off my lap. 'That's for me. But you can have some if you want.'

'Thank you. But I'll have tea.' I get up to take the tray and I look Tracy in the eye. 'Speaking of tea, what did Aggie say when she dropped Eve off?'

Tracy grins. 'I think that should wait until little ears aren't flapping.'

'I'm not listening,' says Eve, sitting on the grass and giving Horatio the bowl of water that Tracy brought out for him on the tray.

'Tell me later.' I lower my voice. 'Eve just asked me if I like her dad. Aggie apparently told Ward he's a fool and that he should tell me, but Eve didn't hear the rest and then later she heard Ward say that I don't like him. I think ... I think she is hoping that something might happen between me and Ward.'

Tracy rolls her eyes. 'We're all hoping that, Geneva.'

'We are? That's news to me.'

'Don't pretend you don't like him. It's obvious you do.'

We sit on the chairs and watch Eve and Horatio.

'Okay, I do. But you said it yourself. Ward knows about me and my money, and he'll do everything he can to stop himself from falling for me. And after the state I was in today, no man would fall for me. But in any event, he doesn't like me. I know you think he does and the way he's looked at me a couple of times, I thought he might, but he doesn't.'

'For an intelligent woman, Geneva, you're behaving like a fool. Which is something similar to what Aggie told Ward. Only he's a man not a woman, obviously.'

'Is that what she told you?'

Tracy nods. 'Yes. I think you and Ward need to have a conversation. And preferably sooner than later.'

'No way. I'm avoiding him.'

Tracy stares at me and raises her brows. 'Why?'

'Because the last thing I want is to fall for someone else right now.'

'Too late for that,' she says. 'That ship has sailed.'

'It wouldn't work.'

'You don't know that.'

'You said he'd fight his feelings.'

'He will.'

'I don't want another man who doesn't want me.'

'Oh he wants you. I'm certain of that. He just needs to realise how much.'

I tut at her. 'You haven't even seen us together. How can you be so sure?'

'Because as I told you, I know Ward, and Roger knows Ward. Now drink your tea and let's go down to the beach.'

'I'm not going anywhere near the ferry.'

'There's plenty of beach away from the ferry.' She stands up and smiles at Eve. 'We're talking of going to the beach, sweetheart. Would you like that?'

Eve jumps up and smiles. 'Yes please. I haven't been to the beach for ages.'

'Erm. Weren't you there yesterday?' I ask. 'Didn't you throw stones in the sea?'

'Uh-huh. That was ages ago,'

'Right,' I say. 'Well that's told me.'

'Can we go and see Dad?' Eve asks as we gather our things together.

'He's working,' I say.

'He's always working,' Eve sighs, adding, 'These days.' And she runs off ahead.

Tracy nods and looks at me. 'Since Roger retired, it's been an extra struggle for Ward. He's been looking for a new ferryman for months, but no one wants to work on a small island ferry all day when they can work on a cruise ship and travel the world.'

'Really? Surely there must be someone on this island who could do it? Or even someone who could help out part time?'

'He's asked everyone. They've offered to help here and there. But no one wants to do it on a permanent basis. Roger says he will return if Ward doesn't find someone soon, and both Ward and I are dreading that. I know Roger loves it but he's simply too old for that sort of work.'

'Is it a question of money?' I ask. 'I mean, is the salary competitive?'

'It's fair. That's not really the problem though. The ferry needs to be moored here overnight, so whoever takes on the job needs to live on the island. They can't get back to the mainland each night without transport, and the ferry is the only transport.'

'Hmm. Eve! We're not going to the beach near the ferry,' I yell as she and Horatio race down the road.

'It seems we are,' says Tracy. 'Unless you want to be the one to tell Ward that we left his daughter on the beach alone with all the Saturday tourists, because you are avoiding him?'

'Funny,' I say. And let out a long sigh. 'Don't expect me to talk to him.'

'Why would you?' Tracy laughs.

Naturally, it is my luck that Ward has recently docked and that he is walking along Boardwalk behind a line of people that he has just brought over on the ferry. I step on to the sandy beach, in the hope I can put some distance between us but Eve has other plans.

'Dad!' Eve shrieks and runs to him, weaving in and out of the crowd of people on

Boardwalk.

He sweeps her up in his arms and spins her round and round as if he hasn't seen her for days. And then he spots Tracy and me and I can see his entire body tense.

He carries Eve under one arm and comes towards us. I turn to run but Tracy grabs my wrist.

'Oh no you don't,' she says. 'Hello Ward! What perfect timing!'

'Hello, Tracy,' he says, smiling at her, as he slides Eve on to her feet, and then he smiles somewhat sheepishly at me. 'Hi, Gen.'

My foolish heart goes all fluttery and colour creeps over my cheeks as I remember the last time he looked at me.

'Hi. We won't disturb you. You've got work to do. And don't worry. I won't climb any trees. Or cliffs. Or anything.'

He clears his throat. 'I think I may owe you an apology.'

I raise my brows. 'Just the one?'

He makes an apologetic face. 'Probably several.'

'Actually, Ward,' Tracy says. 'You do. Now this may not be any of my business, but I know for a fact Geneva climbed Mount Olympus. I saw the photos myself.'

'I told you, Dad,' says Eve, who is now holding Ward's hand.

He runs his free hand through his hair. 'I

know, honey. I'm sorry. I should've believed you.' He looks me in the eye. 'And I should've believed you, too. Roger called me into the tourist office, just before this trip, and showed me the photos on the internet.'

'He did?' I query, surprised and pleased that Roger had stood up for me.

'He did,' says Ward. 'I'm sorry. Forgive me? I shouldn't have assumed that climbing a mountain, was something Geneva McBriar would never do.'

'I'll forgive you, if you'll forgive me for climbing that tree.'

'Already forgiven.'

'Really?'

He nods. 'Really. And thank you.'

'What for?'

'For showing Eve that women can do anything.'

'Now you're being sarcastic.'

'No! I'm honestly not. I mean it. You were right. Eve needs to know that she shouldn't have to call a man to do something if there is a woman who is clearly more than capable of dealing with the situation. Lesson learned. For both Eve and for me.'

'Thank you. That means a great deal.'

'Dad?' says Eve, and I can tell from her tone that's she up to something. 'Are you really sorry?'

'Yes, Eve, I am.'

'Then we must invite Gen for supper tonight, mustn't we? Aunt Aggie says that's the best way to apologise. That and flowers. But you've already bought flowers, haven't you?'

He looks astonished and embarrassed and confused and, perhaps even, a tad cross.

'Don't worry,' I say. 'That's not necessary.'

'It is,' says Eve. 'It would be rude not to. I heard that today.'

I laugh at that.

'Erm. I ... I'm not sure Gen wants to have supper with us, honey.'

'She does,' says Eve.

'Do you?' asks Ward. I may be mistaken but I think there's a hopeful look in his eyes. He ruins it by adding, 'Why don't you and Roger come too, Tracy?'

'Oh that's very kind, Ward, and we'd love to, normally. But sadly, we have already made plans for tonight. I was going to tell Geneva that she would be eating supper on her own, so it's lovely to know that she won't be, and that she'll be having supper with you.'

I know Tracy is lying, but does Ward know?

'I see.' He frowns slightly. 'That's settled then. If you don't mind eating early, you can come home with us when I pick up Eve from

194

Tracy's this evening on my way home. Is that okay with you?'

'Yes. I'll be ready.'

'Good. Erm. I'd better get back to work. The ferry won't sail itself.' He screws up his face as if he wishes he hadn't said that. 'Bye.' He kisses Eve on her head, smiles at me oddly, and marches off the way he came.

'Well,' says Tracy, beaming at Eve and then at me. 'That couldn't have gone better if we'd planned it.'

And by the way she winks at Eve, and Eve winks back, or tries to, I wonder if that's exactly what the pair of them did.

Seventeen

I know precisely what to wear for every occasion – except supper with Ward and Eve.

I have tried on dress after dress, and rejected each one. I'm almost at my wit's end. I'd take the ferry to Folkestone, but then I'd have to explain to Ward that I was going into town to buy a dress for supper tonight with a man I fancy the pants off.

Why aren't there any designer clothes shop on this island?

There is the dressmaker, Esther Dupont on Boardwalk. But even a fairy godmother couldn't get all the creatures on the island to magically spin together a beautiful dress for me in less than an hour, so Esther has no hope.

And then I remember Natalie.

I find the phone number of The Clothing Locker and call it hoping she is working today.

'The Clothing Locker. Natalie speaking. How may I help you?'

'Natalie? It's Gen. The woman with the macs from yesterday.'

'Hello, Gen! How are you?'

'Desperate. Look. I'm sorry about this and I don't have time to explain, but I need a dress in one hour. Less than an hour. Do you have any beautiful, sexy, but not too sexy, classy-looking dresses in the store? Can we Facetime or something and you can use your phone to let me see your stock? Is that possible? I'll make it worth your while.'

'Of course,' she says. 'And you don't need to do that. You were so generous yesterday and I said I'd help in any way I can, if you need me.

'Natalie, you're a life-saver.'

Five minutes later, I've found a dress, paid for it over the phone, and Natalie has arranged for a friend of hers to drop it off at White Cliffs Cottage in ten minutes. I just hope it fits.

Eve is asleep; she is completely worn out, and so are Tracy, and Roger who has returned once again from the tourist office. That place seems to have strange hours.

I look out of my bedroom window and listen to the waves washing up on the sandy shore many feet away, thank heavens. I remember all the day trippers we saw on the

197

beach and all those people on the Boardwalk. And I suddenly have an idea.

I call a man I know, through previous business deals we've done or worked on together, to get some advice and possibly some ballpark figures, but he isn't available so I leave a message. It's Saturday so I probably won't hear from him until Monday, but I'm feeling rather excited. And not just because I'm having supper with Ward tonight.

The dress arrives and I'm almost speechless. It cost about a hundredth of what I would normally pay just for a zip, and yet this dress is beautiful. It's bright red chiffon – which I can live with, and it has a cinched-in waist and a floaty A line skirt with a split from the hem, just above my knees, to an inch below my hip. Both the front and the back have V-shaped necklines plunging to a little above the waist, which means I'll be braless, but that's fine. Like the rest of my body, my boobs are pretty perfect. I've got a black silk stole, a bit like Aggie's, but prettier, and with my black high-heeled sandals and my black evening bag, I'm more than pleased with my appearance.

Judging by the look on Ward's face when I open the door to him at exactly 6.00 p.m., so is he.

'Wow!' he says, his eyes travelling the

length of my body – twice. 'You look stunning.' He glances down at his own clothes. 'I'll shower and change as soon as we're home. Erm. Is Eve ready?'

'I'm here, Dad,' she says sleepily. 'Doesn't Gen look beautiful?'

Ward meets my eyes and holds the look. 'She does. Incredibly so.'

And then he sweeps Eve up and sits her on one hip, with one arm wrapped around her. He holds out his free hand and I place mine in his and with Horatio following close behind, we walk towards Locke Keep, as if we're already a family.

Eighteen

Locke Keep is magnificent outside, despite its crumbling towers, but it's even more so inside. I've seen and stayed in many such places, of course, and even one or two palaces, but walking over the threshold of Locke Keep I experience a sensation I've never had before; I feel as if I've come home.

Wishful thinking? Possibly.

But as Ward shows me the Great Hall, which is more impressive than I'd expected, I genuinely believe I've been here before.

Impossible? Probably.

But the universe itself seems impossible, so who knows?

The walls of the Great Hall are hung with tapestries, hundreds of years old, and the ancient refectory table surrounded by thirty chairs could tell tales of Knights, and Lords and Ladies and Kings and Queens long gone. I close my eyes for a second and it's as if I'm there.

My heels click on the flagstone floor as we walk towards a large staircase to the left of the Great Hall. Portraits of Lockes of old, adorn the staircase walls, and the resemblance of the male-line to Ward is spookily uncanny. It's as if someone has simply copied the same portrait over and over again, and then given each one throughout the ages, a different set of clothes and a hairstyle that were fashionable for that time.

The first floor is where Ward and Eve live now. There's a kitchen, a sitting room and three bedrooms, all of which are welcoming, and decorated and furnished with items appropriate to the surroundings. I wonder if Ward's former wife had had a say in the decoration but as nothing looks as if it has been altered for many years, I seriously doubt it. Homes like these are not renovated on someone's whim, nor redecorated to someone's personal taste. They stand the test of time and nothing much is changed unless it falls down and has to be replaced.

'This is a wonderful home, Ward,' I say, as he lets go of my hand and encourages Eve to stand.

'Thank you,' he says. 'I was hoping you'd think so. I can't imagine living anywhere else. Ever.' He holds my gaze as if he's telling me something that he thinks I need to know.

'If I lived here, I don't think I'd ever want to leave it either.'

He studies my face and a slight frown forms. 'Please don't say that just because you think it's what I want to hear,' he says.

'I'm not! I mean it. Don't take this the wrong way, and you'll think this is ludicrous, but when we first stepped over the threshold, I felt ... as if I belong here. As if I've come home. As if I've been here before. Crazy, right? I've stayed in hundreds of places a bit like this one, but I've never had that feeling.'

He can't seem to take his eyes off me.

'I don't think that's crazy. I ... I felt like that when I held your hand. It was as if it was the most natural thing in the world. As if I'd held hands with you hundreds of times before and our hands just fit perfectly together. That's something I'd never felt before. Not even with my wife. And it scared me half to death.'

'Dad?' Eve says, leaning against him. 'I'm very tired. May I just go to bed?'

'Are you okay, honey?' He focuses all his attention on Eve now.

She nods sleepily. 'Uh-huh. Just sleepy. Sorry Gen.'

'Don't worry about me, Eve. Go to sleep. We'll see one another tomorrow.'

'Don't go, will you?'

'I won't.'

'Promise?'

'Uh-huh.'

'Night then.' Eve yawns and rubs her eyes.

'I'll make sure she's okay, and I'll be back when she's settled,' Ward says. 'Sorry about this. Help yourself to wine. The kitchen is through there. Or to anything else you'd like. I won't be too long.'

'No rush. I'll be here. Waiting.'

He stares at me with an intensity that makes me want to melt into his arms and it's as if he doesn't want to go, but then he sweeps Eve up and carries her to one of the rooms to my left and Horatio hurries after them.

All I can think about is how wonderful it would feel to be swept up into Ward's arms like that and carried off to a bedroom. His bedroom, preferably.

I must stop thinking about sleeping with Ward. Not that I'd have any intention of actually sleeping.

I shake myself and mumble under my breath to pull myself together.

I look around the sitting room and there are photos of him and Eve, photos of Eve and Aggie, and photos of the three of them together, and Horatio of course. That dog goes everywhere Eve goes, it seems. I wonder where he goes when she's at school? There are more photos, some of Ward with a man who is obviously his dad, and with his grandparents. Photos of Roger and Tracy. Photos of lots of people. But no photos, that I can see, of Ward with his former wife.

I wander into the kitchen. It's such a warm and happy room. There are drawings obviously done by Eve, stuck on the walls and the fridge and the windows, and there are more photos of the family and friends, but still none of anyone who might have been his wife. That seems a little odd. But then there was talk of a trial separation and she had died very quickly; perhaps it was still too painful for him. Although it was six years ago.

I walk back into the sitting room and to a large window and stare out over the island, and the cliffs and the sea and to the coast of Folkestone beyond. I have a sense of being watched and I turn slowly to find Ward looking at me from across the room.

'Oh. I didn't hear you come back. Is Eve settled?'

He nods. 'Yes. It's been a hectic day for her. Too much excitement, I think.'

'I know how she feels.'

He looks confused, unsure of himself now.

'Geneva, I ... I'm not sure what's going on here, or if anything is, but I'm sorry for the things I said to you yesterday and today. I did judge you, and that was wrong. And I did assume the worst and that was wrong too. But you need to understand that Eve is the most important person in my life. I can't risk her getting hurt. She's already become closer to you than she has with anyone she's ever known. I don't know how or why that is, but it's happened, and I can't stop that. I don't know if you like me or not. I don't know if you just want to have sex with me and move on. I don't know anything right now. I've never felt this confused, or bewildered or uncertain in my life.'

'I feel the same. Ward. It's not just you.'

'Is this a game. Geneva? If it is, I won't be cross, but I need to know for Eve's sake. I do believe you genuinely like her so please, don't lie to me or pretend. Just give it to me straight.'

'It's not a game. It's not a pretence. And yes, I do like her. Very much. And ... and I also like you.'

'Do you?' He sounds surprised. 'You're beautiful and brilliant, but you're also rich and ruthless. You've got a fantastic life. You can do whatever you want, whenever you want and go wherever you want to go. I'm a struggling, single dad with an ailing ferry business, an ancient crumbling Keep, and more money going out than coming in. Some catch, huh? Plus, I've got an island filled with people I care about. I need to help all the people here keep roofs over their heads and the businesses to get cash into their tills. But most importantly, I have a daughter who means the world to me. I can't risk doing anything that might cause her unhappiness for even a second. I can't bring someone into her life who doesn't intend to stay. I can't fall for someone who wouldn't want to make this island their home.'

'I understand. And I have some ideas that might help with some of that. But we can talk about that another time. Let me get this straight too. Are you saying that you don't just see me as someone you'd like to have sex with? Are you saying you would like this to be something more? Even though you're not really sure if you like me?'

'I'm sure I like you. I'm just not sure why. As I said, you're beautiful, but that isn't what's made me feel like this. It's ... it's something deeper. You said you felt as if you belong here. The crazy thing is, the moment you stepped into my life, it felt as if you belonged there. And if feels as if you belong here. But we seem to keep arguing. And ... and I'm scared. I'll admit that. What if we start something and it goes terribly wrong?'

'It's a risk, I'll admit. But what if we start something and it goes wonderfully right? I didn't come to this island to fall in love or even to have a fling. I told you that yesterday. But I can't seem to get you out of my head or off my mind. Maybe what we should do is sleep together and see how we feel then.'

'That also scares the hell out of me. What if that makes things worse? Or if one of us still wants more but the other doesn't? The main problem for me is that I've never fallen for someone so fast. I knew my wife for years before we married. And even that didn't work out. We ended up as virtual strangers. But I never felt for her what I'm feeling right now. What I've been feeling since the moment you stepped on to my ferry. Can I trust you, Geneva? Are you the woman I think you are? Or are you the Geneva McBriar I've heard and read about? Which one is really you? Because I can't figure it out.'

'I'm not sure myself. I told you I came here to change. But maybe I'm finding myself. All I know is I like you. I like Eve. I like Horatio. I like this island. And I think I could be happy here.'

'After just one day?

'One and a half days really, but yes. Don't forget, as you rightly say, I can go anywhere I want. Anywhere in the world. It seems the only place I want to be, is here. I feel as if I'm home.'

My phone rings and interrupts us.

'Sorry. I'll let it go to voicemail.'

'No. Please answer it. It may be important. I need to shower anyway. As I said earlier, help yourself to anything you want. I won't be long.'

I'm astonished to see it's Francis; the man I'd called earlier and left a message on his voicemail.

'Hello, Francis! Thank you for returning my call, especially on a Saturday night.'

'For you, Geneva? Anything. Besides, I'm waiting for my daughter to arrive, and you know she's always late. How have you been?'

'Erm. Not bad, thanks. But I'm taking a break from the office and ... trying out a few new things. How are you? And how's Lisa?'

'All good here, thanks. What kind of new things?'

'Things that might involve piling into a sandy beach and pouring in several tonnes of concrete. Or something like that. I don't want to put you in an awkward position, but can we keep this between ourselves? I don't want anyone to find out where I am, or what I'm hoping to achieve. But I've got lots of ideas racing around in my head and I'd like some advice and some ballpark figures of costs. Can you help me with that and keep it under wraps?'

'Absolutely.'

I hear a noise from behind but I don't think anything of it. Not until it's too late.

'Thanks, Francis. I'll whizz you across some details over the next few days. Take care. And give my love to your family.'

'So I was right all along!'

When I spin round and face Ward, he not only looks as if his heart has been broken, he looks as if he'd like to kill me. He's taken off his clothes and he's wrapped in a towel, but he's bone dry so he must've come back for something.

'How much of that did you hear?'

'Pretty much all of it. You're really something, Geneva McBriar. You genuinely had me believing you were the woman for me, and that you wanted me as much as I wanted you, but no. It's not me and my body you want to get your hands on, is it? It's my island and my properties? Well good luck with that.'

'You're wrong. Ward! You don't understand. That wasn't what you think it was.'

'Of course it wasn't. Let me save you some time. You're clearly unaware of how this island works. You probably think we're governed by Folkestone and Hythe District Council. But you'd be wrong. This island has been privately owned for centuries. There are restrictive covenants on what can and can't be built here and even who can and can't purchase properties. Residents only, I'm afraid, and UK laws can't change that, because I own this private island and it's in trust for my heirs. An ancient trust that's still binding. What's more, Locke Isle has its own administrative area – just like the Isle of Wight. This is a unitary authority, and I believe, the smallest of its kind in the UK. That means it is responsible for all matters including housing, planning and waste collection together with functions such as transport, social care, and education. Basically anything and everything to keep the island afloat. Excuse the pun. So, Geneva, you can take your piles and your concrete and you can shove them elsewhere. You know where the door is. Close it on your way out. Oh, and you've got two days to get off my island. Because we also have our own police force here, and troublemakers aren't welcome.'

He turns and storms off and I'm left utterly bereft and speechless.

Only this time, I'm not going to walk away.

Nineteen

I am absolutely livid. After all the things he said earlier, the minute he overhears a conversation he jumps to conclusions. I follow him into his bedroom and see he's gone to take his shower in his en suite. That's not going to stop me.

I kick off my shoes and stand beside the long glass panel. He spins round just as I had a few seconds ago, the difference being, he's now stark naked, and despite my fury, I can't help but notice he has the perfect physique.

'What the F–! he says, like a man who is used to stopping himself from cursing in case his child hears. 'Get the hell out of my bathroom!' He tries to cover himself but fails.

I take one more look and then I toss him the towel he has hung on the radiator, and he hastily turns off the shower and wraps the towel around his waist.

'No! You've said your piece now I'll say

mine. They say no man is an island, but you are Ward! You can't seem to think about anything other than this place, except perhaps for Eve. This is your own little Camelot isn't it? And you're the conquering hero. Well, you'll need a bloody magician to keep Locke Isle afloat. And I might've been your Merlin. You said all those things about feelings and wanting me, and seeing a future for us, but the second you think you hear something you don't like, do you pleasantly say, "Geneva? What was that about?" Do you give me the benefit of the doubt? No. You jump to your own conclusions. You start assuming things you shouldn't. You call me names and say how you were right. Well you were wrong. Yet again, Ward.'

'Really? So I didn't hear you say you were planning to put piles and concrete on the sandy beach? There's only one reason for that Geneva. To build one of McBriar Properties famous resorts.'

'You did hear me say that. Exactly that. But you didn't hear why or for what purpose, so I'll tell you. Last night I noticed the stairs in Tracy and Roger's cottage are on the slant. I don't know if it's old settlement or recent. I'd need to have that checked. Or I suppose, now that I know you are in control of everything, I could simply ask you.'

'It's both,' he says.

'I thought it might be. Well, today I saw all those day trippers on the beach and I had an idea. Francis, the man you heard me speaking with owns a company that drills into any terrain and inserts concrete piles, among other stuff, but we'll stick with this for now. The beach here is fantastic but the Boardwalk isn't long enough or wide enough. So I thought, what if I suggested to Ward that a longer and wider Boardwalk could be built? Not only would it mean more shops and businesses along the beachfront. Pop-ups like in Folkestone perhaps, not necessarily permanent buildings. The Boardwalk would bring in more tourists and more money and at the same time another structure could be built behind it to hold back the cliff and to catch any of it that fell. That might protect Tracy and Roger's cottage for many years and all the other cottages along the cliff edge.'

He narrows his eyes and frowns. 'And what would you get out of it?'

'The pleasure of knowing that I had done something nice for my friends. And possibly a free ice cream once in a while. But only when the businesses were all making regular and sustainable profits. But the ice cream is negotiable.'

'What else?'

'Nothing else.'

He snorts derisively. 'That would cost millions, Geneva.'

'I have millions, Ward. Just sitting in my bank account. And other bank accounts elsewhere.'

'And you honestly expect me to believe that you'd do this just for me?'

'Oh no. Not just for you. For Tracy and for Roger, mainly, but it would be nice if it helped you too. I had another idea as well.'

'I bet you did.'

'You're doing it again, Ward. You're judging me and assuming. My idea is about the ferry.'

'Keep your hands off the ferry.'

'I intend to. Tracy says the ferryman must live on the island. But he, or she, doesn't need to. Not if there is another boat. A smaller boat. One that the ferryman could take back to Folkestone or wherever and moor for the night and then come back to the island the next day. And better yet, that smaller boat could be like the water taxis in Venice. Have you been to Venice?'

'No.'

'We must go there then. You'll need to see them. Anyway, the water taxi could also take passengers to and fro but at a much lower cost than it takes for the ferry to go to and fro. Just an idea.'

'And how would we find the money for

another boat?'

I point at myself.

'You're saying you'd also buy this boat? For nothing in return?'

'Ah. I might expect the odd free crossing. Assuming I'm not chucked off the island, that is.'

'Are you … are you serious? Is this … is this really the truth? Can I honestly trust you?'

'Yes, Ward. You can. Why is that so hard for you to believe?'

'Because I trusted my wife. And she had an affair behind my back. Two affairs in fact. I forgave the first, but not the second. We were planning to separate and divorce and then she … fell ill. I couldn't let her die alone, could I? But I've found it hard to trust anyone since. Especially beautiful women.'

'Oh I'm sorry, Ward! I didn't know!'

He smirks suddenly. 'I didn't tell you, so I suppose that's my fault. Sorry. I didn't tell anyone.'

'Right. Well. I've said what I had to say. If you still want me to go, I'll go. But I meant what I said, Ward. I do like it here and I do want to stay, if you'll let me.'

'And pay for everything to save the island?' He shakes his head. 'I don't think I could let you do that. What if you lost every penny?'

'What if I didn't? And even if I did. You said yourself that money doesn't buy happiness. I heard you tell Eve that yesterday. And I can confirm it's true. It hasn't bought me happiness. But some concrete piles and a small boat, might.'

He grins at me. 'And what about us? Assuming there might still be an 'us' after me being such a bloody idiot yet again. What if things don't work out? I'd never be able to repay you and you'd never be able to get your money back?'

'I can always make more. The thing about money is that when you have it, it seems to accumulate. It's usually only when you're struggling that you seem to let it slip through your fingers. Are you saying you'd still like there to be an 'us'?'

He looks me in the eyes for what seems like a long, long time.

'Yes.'

'Good. Because I've got a few more ideas to bring money and tourists to the island and I think we should discuss them at some stage soon.'

'I can't wait to hear them. And I promise I will try to never jump to conclusions again. Now may I please take my shower?'

I look him up and down and smile. 'Yes. But there's one more thing I need to say. Because you were completely wrong about that too.'

'I was? What was that?'

'It's not your properties and your island I want to get my hands on, Ward Locke. It is most definitely you and your body. And I want to get my hands on them right now.'

I pull the towel from around his waist and he stands naked in front of me for a moment, and then he smiles at me and his eyes light up.

'I think that's one deal that won't require any negotiation,' he says. 'I've been longing to get my hands on you and your body since you stepped on my ferry.'

He pulls me into the shower with him and he kisses me as if he will never let me go.

I have no idea what our futures may hold, but I think I can safely say that whatever it is, we'll be holding on to each other.

Twenty

A few days later, I'm sitting in White Cliffs Café with Tracy and discussing plans for the future.

'Paint me green and call me a cucumber!' Sylvie says, as her sister Cece places a tray of coffees and cakes before her. Sylvie is leaning on her elbows on the counter, reading a newspaper and pushes herself upright, pointing at the paper as she does so. Cece peers over her shoulder and tuts.

'Deary me. I wouldn't want to be in her shoes.'

'Or in the audience,' adds Sylvie. 'I bet they got more than they bargained for.'

The sisters chuckle like wicked witches and then Sylvie tucks the paper under her arm and carries the tray to our table.

'Look at that headline,' she says, dropping the paper without using her hands. 'The "Beach Baby" one.' She slides the tray on to the table pushing the paper forwards.

Tracy picks it up and reads it aloud. 'Pop Princess, Lucinda Revere gave her audience a lot more than her top hits, at the second of the open-air festivals she has headlined at this summer. Seascape Café and Norman Landing Beach Concert...' Tracy trails off and looks at me.

'Don't stop there!' Sylvie orders, and grabs the paper from Tracy's hands, repeating those last few words and continuing to read the rest of the article. '"Seascape Café and Norman Landing Beach Concert has garnered many ardent fans since its first offering at the end of July, and fans of both the concert and of Lucinda, were eager to bag tickets for this August Bank Holiday Weekend Extravaganza. But no one expected quite how much Lucinda would be sharing with her devoted fans. We all knew she was pregnant. She announced that news at New Year when she and her new husband, the former World Cup Ski Champion, Cody Clayton told the world of their secret Winter Wedding in the Bavarian Alps, and dropped the bombshell that Cody was retiring from competitive skiing. And those attending the July, Seascape Café and Norman Landing Beach Concert, saw how huge Lucinda was, but the baby wasn't due for another two weeks. Some people criticised her for performing on stage in front of a huge audience when she was so heavily pregnant, but Lucinda joked that she would continue giving her fans what they wanted, even if it meant delivering her baby in her dressing room. Never was a truer word spoken – although she didn't make it back to the dressing room. She was belting out a sensational performance of her brand new hit single, the aptly named, 'Baby, This is a Surprise', when her waters broke on Saturday evening. And what a surprise everyone was in for! Cody was the first to rush to the pop icon's aid, followed closely by friends and staff of the recently opened music venue, Seascape Café. But the baby, who is clearly intending to follow in his mother's footsteps, didn't want to wait, and Lucinda gave birth to a healthy, baby boy, right there on the stage, with a spectacular sunset as a backdrop, and a crowd of thousands cheering and screaming and wondering what was going on, as screens were hastily placed around Lucinda to respect her privacy. Mother and baby were then taken to the local hospital in Brighton and we're delighted to report both are fit and healthy. A true trooper, even at such a time, Lucinda asked her fans, via a statement from her manager, to forgive her for rushing away mid-concert, and everyone who attended will be given a free ticket to Lucinda's next performance, although we have no dates for that, as yet. Her husband Cody said they're both thrilled, and Lucinda will be back, performing before too long, but she does intend to take some time off now to be with her family. No name has been given, yet, for the baby who couldn't wait to be a star. We all wish Lucinda, Cody and Star Baby, every happiness for the future." Well,' says Sylvie, looking at Tracy and me, 'what do you think of that?'

'I think it's a shame the details are plastered all over the newspapers,' Tracy says. 'But I wish them the best of everything.'

'Me too,' I say, picturing Mack and Tori, and no doubt Emma Barr, and all the rest of their friends, rushing to Lucinda's side. I know Tracy stopped reading because she was concerned it would bring back painful memories for me, but oddly enough, other than the initial shock of hearing the café mentioned, remembering Mack, and picturing them all, I only feel happiness for Lucinda and her husband. Probably because I've finally found happiness myself. 'Rather her than me,' I add.

Sylvie nods. 'I wouldn't want everyone seeing me give birth.' She chuckles. 'Mind you, at my age, that would definitely make the front page. It'd be a major miracle.'

She shakes her head, stuffs the newspaper back under her arm and saunters off to the kitchen, leaving me and Tracy sipping our coffees.

'It's arrived,' the door bursts open and Eve rushes in, followed closely by Horatio, and finally by Ward.

He smiles at me and comes over and kisses me on the lips. 'The new boat has arrived,' he says. 'In case you didn't hear Eve yelling that all the way here. Are you going to come and see it?

'Absolutely,' I say. 'And I've had another idea.'

'Great news,' he says. 'Oddly enough, so have I. But it can wait for a while.'

He gently pulls me to my feet and into his arms and then, just before his lips meet mine, he whispers, 'I love you, Geneva McBriar.'

Taking a break was the best decision I have ever made.

I can't wait to see Dad's face when I tell him.

Especially when I add that I won't be going back to work at McBriar Properties, and I'm selling my apartment in Edinburgh.

I have a new home now and it's filled with happiness and love ... and a large and comfy sofa, that's seen better days, but that's big enough for me, and Ward and Eve and

Horatio to curl up on, together, each and every day.

Coming soon

Visit www.emilyharvale.com to see
what's coming next.

Plus, sign up for Emily's newsletter, or join
her Facebook group, for all the latest news
about her books.

Stay in touch with

Emily Harvale

Sign up for Emily's newsletter to find out about book releases, see covers, help name characters or pick book titles, enter giveaways and lots more.

Go to www.emilyharvale.com to sign up.

Or join her Facebook group for all of the above and to chat with Emily and others about her books:

www.emilyharvale.com/FacebookGroup

Alternatively, say 'Hello' on social media:

 @EmilyHarvaleWriter

 @EmilyHarvale

 @EmilyHarvale

A Note from Emily

Thank you for reading this book. I really hope it brought a smile to your face. If so, I'd love it if you'd leave a short review on Amazon, or even just a rating.
And, maybe, tell your friends, or mention it on social media.

A little piece of my heart goes into all my books. I can't wait to bring you more stories that I hope will capture your heart, mind and imagination, allowing you to escape into a world of romance in some enticingly beautiful settings.

To see my books, or to sign up for my newsletter, please visit my website. The link is on the previous page.

I love chatting to readers, so pop over to Facebook or Instagram and say, 'Hello'. Or better yet, there's my lovely Facebook group for the latest book news, chats and general book-related fun. Again, you'll find details on the previous page.

Also by Emily Harvale

The Golf Widows' Club
Sailing Solo
Carole Singer's Christmas
Christmas Wishes
A Slippery Slope
The Perfect Christmas Plan
Be Mine
It Takes Two
Bells and Bows on Mistletoe Row

Lizzie Marshall series:
Highland Fling – book 1
Lizzie Marshall's Wedding – book 2

Goldebury Bay series:
Ninety Days of Summer – book 1
Ninety Steps to Summerhill – book 2
Ninety Days to Christmas – book 3

Hideaway Down series:
A Christmas Hideaway – book 1
Catch A Falling Star – book 2
Walking on Sunshine – book 3
Dancing in the Rain – book 4

Hall's Cross series
Deck the Halls – book 1
The Starlight Ball – book 2

Michaelmas Bay series
Christmas Secrets in Snowflake Cove – book 1
Blame it on the Moonlight – book 2

Norman Landing series
Saving Christmas – book 1
A not so secret Winter Wedding – book 2
Sunsets and Surprises at Seascape Café – book 3
A Date at the end of The Pier – book 4

To see a complete list of my books, or to sign up for my newsletter, go to
www.emilyharvale.com/books

There's also an exclusive Facebook group for fans of my books.
www.emilyharvale.com/FacebookGroup

Or scan the QR code below to see all my books on Amazon.

Printed in Great Britain
by Amazon

26828011R00142